Writing Tricksters

Writing Tricksters

Mythic Gambols in American Ethnic Literature

Jeanne Rosier Smith

810.
9
SM6

University of California Press

Berkeley   Los Angeles   London

University of California Press
Berkeley and Los Angeles, California

University of California Press, Ltd.
London, England

© 1997 by
The Regents of the University of California

Library of Congress Cataloging-in-Publication Data

Smith, Jeanne Rosier, 1966–
    Writing tricksters : mythic gambols in American ethnic literature / Jeanne Rosier
Smith.
        p.   cm.
    Includes bibliographic references (p.) and index
    ISBN 0-520-20654-1 (alk. paper).—ISBN 0-520-20656-8 (pbk. : alk. paper)
1. American fiction—Women authors—History and criticism.   2. Trickster in literature.
3. American prose literature—20th century—Minority authors—History and criticism.
4. American prose literature—20th century—History and criticism.   5. Literature and
folklore—United States—History—20th century.   6. Women and literature—United
States—History—20th century.   7. Kingston, Maxine Hong—Criticism and interpretation.   8. Erdrich, Louise—Criticism and interpretation.   9. Morrison, Toni—Criticism
and interpretation.   10. Kingston, Maxine Hong. Woman warrior.   11. Minority women
in literature.   12. Ethnic groups in literature.   13. Ethnicity in literature.   14. Narration
(Rhetoric)   I. Title.
PS374.T7S45   1997
   813´95409352—dc20 96–20038
Printed in the United States of America
9   8   7   6   5   4   3   2   1

The paper used in this publication meets the minimum requirements of American National
Standards for Information Sciences—Permanence of Paper for Printed Library Materials,
ANSI Z39.48–1984.

For Brian, Ben, and Katherine

CONTENTS

PREFACE

The germ of this book came from a conference I attended on Asian American women writers at Tufts University in 1990. The keynote speaker, Maxine Hong Kingston, read from her new book, *Tripmaster Monkey*, and Amy Ling delivered a paper on the positive, adaptive trickster strategies of the Eaton sisters, also known as Onoto Watanna and Sui Sin Far. Having just read Louise Erdrich's *Love Medicine*, I was struck by the recurrence of so many trickster figures. I thought of Leslie Silko's *Storyteller*, Erdrich's *Tracks*, and Toni Morrison's *Tar Baby*. Was it coincidence that many of America's most successful and important contemporary women writers were writing tricksters? Why are tricksters—from the Signifying Monkey to Nanabozho to Br'er Rabbit to Coyote to the Monkey King—such a ubiquitous phenomenon?

The trickster's pervasiveness parallels the growth of ethnic literatures in America. The past thirty years have witnessed a tremendous literary and cultural revolution: Native American, African American, Chinese American, and Chicano and Chicana literatures (to name a few) are prospering; multiculturalism has exploded traditional canons; and the borders and boundaries of "American" literature continually fluctuate and blur. Tricksters shake things up, splinter the monologic, shatter the hierarchies. At this new crisis (or carnival) of American literature, tricksters proliferate, disrupting tradition and mediating change.

Tricksters defy homogenization. They cannot be reduced to a lowest common cultural denominator; they only make sense embedded in a cultural context. Perhaps this is why most studies of the trickster, such as John W. Roberts's *From Trickster to Badman*, Robert Pelton's *Trickster in West Africa*, and Paul Radin's classic *The Trickster* focus exclusively on a particular trickster tradition. Similarly, most studies of ethnic literatures recognize and define a specific, shared cultural and literary tradition. Yet despite each ethnic tradition's distinctness and each trickster's cultural particularity, the works of Kingston, Erdrich, and Morrison make abundantly clear that our world does not divide into neat academic categories. Contemporary trickster novels depict a chaotic, multilingual, many-layered world of colliding and overlapping cultures: Kingston's tricksters are railway workers and Berkeley beatniks; Erdrich's tricksters go to Jesuit schools, play bingo, and eat Slim Jims; and Morrison's tricksters bootleg liquor, drink Evian, and model for *Elle*. Though each author draws on a specific tradition, their tricksters revel in the hazardous complexity of life in modern America.

Relatively little literary scholarship to date has looked across cultures toward lines of contact and intersection; few works discuss specifically the links among ethnic writers. We need models of successful cross-cultural negotiation, which allow for points of exchange and intersection across racial, cultural, and ethnic divides, without obliterating or oversimplifying differences. This book is a contribution toward that effort, bringing together major African American, Asian American, and Native American writers under the rubric of the trickster.

All sorts of interesting parallels appear when we consider trickster works cross-culturally: the dynamic function of myth in contemporary ethnic literature, the importance of oral traditions to cultural and individual survival, the multivocal challenge to a unified perspective, and the unusual demands made on the reader. Each of these elements shapes the trickster novel and challenges readers' ways of viewing the world.

The writers considered here celebrate myth and folklore as a vital, dynamic, culturally renewing force. Tricksters, who combine tradition and change, make ideal agents for a politically engaged, visionary art. Central to the nonwestern storytelling traditions on which Kingston, Erdrich, and Morrison draw, the androgynous trickster is infinitely changeable, ancient, and yet perpetually new.

Interpreter, storyteller, and transformer, the trickster is a master of borders and exchange, injecting multiple perspectives to challenge all that is stultifying, stratified, bland, or prescriptive. Tricksters embody the complexity, diversity, and paradoxes of literary studies today, which demand the recognition of competing voices. In multicultural debates, trickster is a lively, diverse, unpredictable, vital actor, enlivening postmodern discourse and everyday lives. It is no accident that many contemporary writers and critics call upon the trickster in their expression of contemporary life and thought. Trickster is a profoundly cross-cultural and therefore truly American phenomenon.

ACKNOWLEDGMENTS

I would like to thank Elizabeth Ammons for her example, inspiration, guidance, and encouragement throughout the writing of this book. Thanks also to Ken Roemer, my ghost adviser, and to Kathleen Allana Brown, Marsha Fulsom, Ruth Hsiao, Clyde Taylor, and the other readers who offered timely advice and suggestions that helped to shape this book. Finally, thanks to Brian, for everlasting patience, faith, and comic relief, and to my mother and father, for showing me the courage and grace in humor.

CHAPTER ONE

The Trickster Aesthetic
A Cross-Cultural Feminist Theory

Through the stories everything is made possible.
Yellowman, Navaho storyteller

Tricksters—the ubiquitous shape-shifters who dwell on borders, at crossroads, and between worlds—are the world's oldest, and newest, creations. Long familiar in folklore as Coyote, Anansi, Hermes, Iktomi, Maui, Loki, Monkey, Nanabozho, and Br'er Rabbit (to name a few), tricksters abound in contemporary American literature, especially in works by women of color. Consider the titles of three recent critical works by women of color: Amy Ling's *Between Worlds: Women Writers of Chinese Ancestry*, Gloria Anzaldúa's *Borderlands/La Frontera: The New Mestiza*, and Paula Gunn Allen's "'Border Studies': The Intersection of Gender and Color." Between worlds, borderlands, border studies— this common emphasis on straddling borders, or existing within or between them, evokes the trickster strategies many women of color are developing in their lives and their writing. Tricksters appear prominently in recent novels by contemporary women of color: Maxine Hong Kingston's *Woman Warrior* (1976), *China Men* (1980), and *Tripmaster Monkey* (1989); Toni Morrison's *Sula* (1972), *Song of Solomon* (1977), and *Tar Baby* (1981); and Louise Erdrich's *Love Medicine* (1993), *The Beet Queen* (1986), *Tracks* (1988), and *The Bingo Palace* (1994). All focus on trickster characters and invent tricksterlike narrative forms. The trickster's resurgence in the fiction and the criticism of women writers of color suggests that the age-old trickster has not lost relevance in the modern world; rather, the trickster has become a key figure for personal and cultural survival in twentieth-century America.

In virtually all cultures, tricksters are both folk heroes and wanderers on the edges of the community, at once marginal and central to the culture. Tricksters challenge the status quo and disrupt perceived boundaries. Whether foolishly, arrogantly, or bravely, tricksters face the monstrous, transforming the chaotic to create new worlds and new cultures. In doing so, they offer appealing strategies to women writers of color who, historically subjugated because of both their race and their sex, often combine a feminist concern for challenging patriarchy with a cultural interest in breaking racial stereotypes and exploring a mixed cultural heritage. Erdrich, Kingston, and Morrison situate the trickster as a key figure in their explorations of culture, gender, and identity. In their novels, tricksters serve to combat racial and sexual oppression and to affirm and create personal and cultural identity. Tricksters are not only characters, they are also rhetorical agents. They infuse narrative structure with energy, humor, and polyvalence, producing a politically radical subtext in the narrative form itself.

◎

My discussion of literary tricksters assumes that neither literature nor literary criticism can be separated from its historical and cultural contexts.[1] Whereas much of the theory surrounding archetypal figures such as the trickster emphasizes the universality or timelessness of myth, my approach follows Estella Lauter's contention that myth is "part of the dynamic of history instead of being one of its reservoirs" (3).[2] In a study of the trickster in the African American tradition, John W. Roberts situates the argument for a dynamic theory of myth in a multicultural context. He calls for culture-specific models in the study of mythic or folk literature and argues that viewing western mythic traditions as universal "turns out to be extremely narrow and ethnocentric, especially . . . in the American context" (4). Mythic and folkloric figures such as the trickster play a crucial role in building and transforming culture; these figures are especially likely to appear when the culture's values or prosperity are threatened, either internally or externally. Myths, then, as they appear in literature, can be read as part of an effort for human and cultural survival. The trickster's role as survivor and transformer, creating order from chaos, accounts for the figure's universal appeal and its centrality to the mythology and folklore of so many cultures.[3] Critic and creator, the trickster challenges culture from both within and without, strengthening and renewing it with outrageous laughter.[4]

The primacy that Erdrich, Kingston, and Morrison place on community and culture puts their work in a genre that Sandra Zagarell has recently identified as the "narrative of community," whose key features include double-voicedness, the primacy of relationships, and ties to tradition (510).[5] The focus of narratives of community helps to clarify their usefulness to the trickster narratives of Erdrich, Kingston, and Morrison. Tricksters, whose polyvalence and multivocality make them emblematic of the intersection of voices, play a central role in the connection of self and culture. Zagarell explains that in contrast to conventional narratives that place primary emphasis on the individual, narratives of community seek "to represent what gives the community its identity, what enables it to remain itself. . . . Writers understood communities to take form through negotiation among diverse, often recalcitrant components—people living at distances from each other; sometimes reluctant individuals; scarce resources; values, practices and lore that are threatened by time and change" (520).

Zagarell identifies time and change as threats to community; to those I would add persecution, immigration laws, relocation, enslavement, and genocide. Zagarell's description of the aims of narratives of community recalls Roberts's description of mythic literature as culture-building and as a continuing, dynamic response to cultural threat. Like Roberts, Zagarell emphasizes a recursive, nonlinear narrative structure: "narratives proceed episodically; the particular sequence of episodes is generally less important than the episodes' repeated exemplification of the dynamics that maintain the community" (520). The parallels between Roberts's and Zagarell's analyses are significant. Although Roberts's analysis focuses on myth and folklore, whereas Zagarell's concerns the daily life of the community, the goal in each case is the preservation and transformation of a shared culture that is threatened by destructive, chaotic forces. This is clearly an aim in the works of Erdrich, Kingston, and Morrison, and the similarities in Roberts's and Zagarell's descriptions of the process of community building suggest a clear link among cultural creation and preservation, the trickster, and the narrative form of these works.[6]

Writing a contemporary mythic novel involves not only recalling traditional stories but also revising them and even creating new ones, a strategy often associated with women's writing.[7] Yet "woman" is not the only, nor even necessarily the most important, group identity of concern to Kingston, Erdrich, and Morrison. Histories of enslavement, relocation, and persecution make ethnicity at least as salient a concern as gender to women writers of color. Reflecting these multiple concerns, Kingston, Erdrich, and Morrison engage in several types of revisionist mythmaking. As they draw on Chinese legend, Chippewa myth, and African American folktale, they not only question gender roles but also revise the traditional myths both of their ancestral backgrounds and of the dominant culture, to suit the needs of life in modern America. With trickster energy, they revise myth, history, and narrative form to simultaneously draw on, challenge, and transform their cultures.

In much American feminist criticism, the recent growth of mythic themes in women's fiction is linked to political ambivalence or escapism. Rita Felski suggests that a concern with myth and spirituality in women's fiction often tends toward "a mystification of femininity and an uncritical celebration of irrationalism," a retreat "backward and inward" so as to escape a patriarchal public history from which women have been excluded (149). Annis Pratt similarly ascribes the use of cyclical plots, myth, and the surreal in women's fiction to their "alienation from normal concepts of time and space" (11).[8]

However, to read the use of myth and cyclical time as abnormal or escapist is to assume that a western, linear, empirical worldview is "normal." Kingston, Erdrich, and Morrison's trickster texts work against such a concept and toward a version of reality that derives from both within and outside of the western ethos. In doing so, they redefine myth and identity and create new novelistic forms to express their vision. Their writing is anything but escapist. As Toni Morrison explains, novels are political, and they function as a modern way of keeping communal stories alive:

> We don't live in places where we can hear those stories anymore; parents don't sit around and tell their children those classical, mythological archetypal stories that we heard years ago. But new information has got to get out, and there are several ways to do it. One is the novel. . . . It should be beautiful, but it should also *work*. It should have something in it that enlightens; something in it that opens the door and points the way. Something in it that suggests what the conflicts are. ("Rootedness" 341)

Morrison's emphasis on "new information" highlights an important feature of the function of myth in these novels. If we see myth as a dynamic production of culture, then new information is vital to the continued life of the myth. Erdrich, Kingston, and Morrison use myth and folklore extensively as part of this continuing process of building a culture and an identity.

In bringing these writers and works together in a comparative study, I do not intend to equate the widely different histories and experiences of three diverse American ethnic groups. Even apparently shared oppressions arise from differing historical conditions, and my subsequent chapters attend to the traditions from which each author writes.[9] Erdrich, Morrison, and Kingston's coinciding concern with the trickster stretches across three figures: Nanabozho, Br'er Rabbit, and Monkey. Grouping these highly disparate tricksters in one study requires creating a discursive space where their similarities can intersect without obliterating their distinctiveness. Tricksters invent culture and demand culturally specific analysis. Yet the "cultures" of the late-twentieth-century authors in this study intersect and overlap, and I would argue that the common focus on tricksters in the works of Erdrich, Kingston, and Morrison suggests kindred impulses toward challenging the possibility of a unified perspective, disrupting perceived histories of oppression, and creating new narrative forms.[10]

◎

Though I attend later to important differences in the origins and development of trickster figures in Native American, Chinese American, and African American traditions, it is nevertheless useful here to sketch out several characteristics that most tricksters share. Victor Turner calls tricksters "liminal phenomena" and maintains that their wide presence in world literatures derives from their liminality, the "betwixt and between" state of transition and change that is a source of myth in all cultures ("Myth and Symbol" 580).[11] As liminal beings, tricksters dwell at crossroads and thresholds and are endlessly multifaceted and ambiguous. Tricksters are uninhibited by social constraints, free to dissolve boundaries and break taboos. Perpetual wanderers, tricksters can escape virtually any situation, and they possess a boundless ability to survive. It is these last two qualities that make the trickster not simply a figure to laugh at but also a hero. Even while transgressing all boundaries, trickster always confirms a human and cultural will to survive.[12]

We cannot—nor would we want to—capture this slippery figure categorically, a fact that has long frustrated and mystified western scholars. Tricksters' lewdness and amorality have led to a negative perception of them as selfish, untrustworthy, and deceitful. Certainly, tricksters often are just that, but they also give life, teach survival, and define culture. In one figure, the trickster unites the sacred and the profane. Because western thought tends to separate honesty and goodness from deception and evil, tricksters, who comically unite opposites and upend categories and conventions, seem shocking, sensational, and morally bankrupt.[13] However, a glance at trickster traditions of Native American, African, and other nonwestern cultures reveals quite a different picture. Despite their apparent marginality and irreverence, tricksters are central, sacred, and communal figures in most nonwestern traditions. Though often bawdy and even anarchic, trickster tales teach through comic example and define culture by transgressing its boundaries. It may only be a western aversion to paradox and disorder, then, that so distorts the trickster's image in the popular imagination.

Despite our supposed disapproval, the trickster has long played a vital role in American literary history. Most studies of tricksters in American literature focus on the nineteenth-century confidence man.[14] William Lenz, discussing Poe, Melville, Twain, and others, calls the con-man "a distinctly American version" of the trickster, setting his birth as a literary convention in the 1830s and 1840s "flush times," when American expansion west fueled dreams of a new country full of potentially exploitable possibilities (1).[15] According to Lenz's model, the con-man as literary convention dies out by the twentieth century, as the closing of the frontier constrains his speculative schemes.

Yet although the confidence man may have begun to disappear, other tricksters—those drawn from African American, Native American, Chicano and Chicana, and Asian American traditions—flourished in the early twentieth century, as writers of color began publishing fiction in greater numbers than ever before. Elizabeth Ammons and Annette White-Parks's collection, *Tricksterism in Turn-of-the-Century American Literature: A Multicultural Perspective*, uncovers trickster strategies in the works of writers such as Charles Chesnutt, Sui Sin Far, Mourning Dove, Zitkala-Ša, and Frances E. W. Harper. For many turn-of-the-century writers, tricksters and trickster strategies represented the most viable way of negotiating the white, male-dominated American publishing industry: "Finding a style in which to write and get published required accommodating the monolithic, racist views of White America. For writers committed to their own people, it also required breaking through them. Such a transaction could only be handled covertly, or by finding strategies to negotiate with a dual audience. . . . From these circumstances . . . 'tricksterism' emerged" (Ammons and White-Parks 16). Unlike the peculiarly western, individually motivated, nineteenth-century confidence man, who never attained the mythic power held by tricksters in cultures with strong oral traditions,[16] tricksters for turn-of-the-century writers of color retain many nonwestern elements, including strong communal values.

True to their role as culture builders, tricksters appear at moments of identity crisis in American literature. In the mid–nineteenth century, with the nation's constitution and borders in flux, writers such as Poe, Melville, and Twain searched for something distinctly American and focused on the wandering con-artist, who flourished on the frontier border towns and outposts precisely because of his or her fluid, ambiguous identity. Turn-of-the-century writers drew on trickster traditions to forge an identity and a writing voice out of clashing cultures and contradictory worlds. Trickster strategies such as masking have always been an integral part of American culture; Ralph Ellison points out that masking is "in the American grain" (55). Recalling Benjamin Franklin's self-presentation as a self-made man, Hemingway's sportsman pose, and Faulkner's farmer persona, Ellison says, "America is a land of masking jokers. We wear the mask for purposes of aggression as well as for defense; when we are projecting the future and preserving the past. In short, the motives hidden behind the mask are as numerous as the ambiguities the mask conceals" (55).

The resurgence of tricksters in contemporary, multicultural literature owes much in spirit to turn-of-the-century tricksterism as political resistance and creative expression.[17] Yet today's publishing industry and reading public are radically different from those at the turn of the century, and constructions of tricksterism have changed. African American, Asian American, Native American, Chicano and Chicana, and other literatures are thriving, exposing the narrowness and inadequacy of traditional canons.[18] The trickster's resurgence on the literary landscape signals a new crossroads in American literature and identity. The works of Leslie Silko, Sandra Cisneros, Gerald Vizenor, Ishmael Reed, and David Henry Hwang, to name a few, clearly demand trickster readings. As tricksters increasingly surface in contemporary multicultural American literature and critical discourse, their historical presence in American literature will no doubt emerge as an important topic for critical attention. At the turn into the twenty-first century, tricksters are everywhere. Tricksters—multiform, disruptive, contradictory, boundary-crossing, parti-colored, and multilingual—define our national character.

Just as tricksters redefine American culture, they reinvent narrative form. The trickster's medium is words. A parodist, joker, liar, con-artist, and storyteller, the trickster fabricates believable illusions with words—and thus becomes author and embodiment of a fluid, flexible, and politically radical narrative form. Viewing the trickster as a rhetorical principle provides a useful framework for analyzing narrative structure in the works of Erdrich, Morrison, and Kingston. The narrative forms of their works share certain distinctive features: breaks, disruptions, loose ends, and multiple voices or perspectives. Current French feminist theory describes such narrative features as part of an *écriture feminine*, which connects a "feminine" style of writing to the female body. However, this view of narrative form is inadequate to a reading of Erdrich, Kingston, and Morrison. In the words of Ann Jones, "It flattens out the lived differences among women. To the extent that each of us responds to a particular tribal, national, racial, or class situation vis-à-vis men, we are in fact separated from one another" (371).[19] Because an analysis of narrative form in the works of Kingston, Erdrich, and Morrison must account not just for the sex of their authors but also for their entire cultural context, the disruptions, spaces, and multiple voices in their narratives can most appropriately be understood in terms of what I call a "trickster aesthetic," which challenges an ethnocentric as well as a phallocentric tradition.

My contention that trickster novels challenge ethnocentrism draws on Mikhail Bakhtin's conception of the novel as "dialogized heteroglossia," or a diversity of points of view in conflict with one another. The interacting languages within the novel represent a freeing of diverse voices from "the hegemony of a single and unitary language" (Bakhtin 366).[20] As various social languages interact—through the characters' speeches, through changes in narrative voice, and through shifts in point of view—the novel form itself decentralizes any single worldview, presenting a potential challenge to ethnocentricity. With masks, laughter, and freedom from social laws and inhibitions, tricksters incarnate the carnivalesque. Tricksters have played a pivotal role in the multivocal, decentralizing aspects of the novel from its beginnings. Bakhtin traces the origins of the novel to the "current of decentralizing, centrifugal forces" found in parodic genres associated with the rogue, fool, and clown—all versions of the trickster.[21] A chief value of parody is in exposing any one perspective, or any one language, as necessarily limited. Tricksters can parody languages, and therefore worldviews, because of their liminal cultural position. Their location outside the confines of rigid social structures gives them a privileged perspective. In the novel, the ever-wandering trickster embodies a "linguistic homelessness" that results in "a verbal and semantic decentering of the ideological world" (Bakhtin 366). When trickster emerges as an active agent within the text, the dismantling of controlling ideologies becomes a key issue. Trickster authors privilege multivocality in order to emphasize that each perspective is different and cannot be eclipsed by an "absolute" perspective.

The political value that the trickster aesthetic places on multiple languages resembles features of *écriture feminine*. Diane

Price Herndl notices striking similarities between Bakhtin's theories of novelistic discourse and theories of a feminine language, observing that both "describe a multivoiced or polyphonic resistance to hierarchies and laughter at authority" (11). Price Herndl's description of feminine writing sounds strikingly tricksterlike: "A feminine language lives on the boundary. A feminine text overthrows the hierarchies. . . . It proves the hierarchies mistaken. Like the voices Bakhtin hears in the novel's carnival, the female voice laughs in the face of authority" (11). Price Herndl advocates a dialogic feminist criticism that "would resist offering 'a reading' and offer, instead, 'readings,'" emphasizing the polyphonic features of texts (18). She admits, however, that "at some point the political need for strategic readings may well outweigh the desire to escape monological, hierarchical ways of thinking and writing" (19). Indeed, it is largely this political need that determines my choice of a trickster aesthetic over a feminine language for analysis of narrative form in Erdrich, Kingston, and Morrison. These writers seek to upset hierarchies not just because they have an inherent philosophical "feminine" dislike for binary oppositions, but because they pursue specific, racially and ethnically grounded sociopolitical purposes. It is the trickster's political exploitation of the carnival that makes the figure so attractive to these writers.

Although trickster tales can, and often do, offer a socially sanctioned way of institutionalizing rebellion in order to reinforce political and cultural norms (as when the tales teach morals through negative example), trickster also inherently questions the limits of order and thus carries the potential for radical (re)vision. As Andrew Wiget explains, "Trickster functions not so much to call cultural categories into question as to demonstrate the artificiality of culture itself. Thus he makes available for discussion the very basis of social order, individual and communal identity" (94). Trickster's challenge to established order shows the limits of any social or political system and thereby prepares the way for creative change and adaptation. In both substance and subtext, contemporary trickster novels disrupt readers' comfortable worldviews and enable us to glimpse new possibilities.[22]

My trickster aesthetic envisions the trickster not only as an actual figure in the novel but also as a linguistic and stylistic principle. Two recent studies of the trickster have isolated the rhetorical as its principal terrain and clarified the connection between narrative form and ideological context. Henry Louis Gates Jr. locates the black English vernacular roots of the African American literary tradition in the African trickster Esu-Elegbara, whose African American descendant, the signifying monkey, continually outwits his foes with skillful stories and verbal barrage. The signifying monkey's power and identity lie in his mastery of verbal technique: "The monkey is not only a master of technique, he *is* technique" (*Signifying* 54). Gerald Vizenor similarly emphasizes the Native American trickster's relationship to form and style, translating the trickster's characteristics into features of language that make up what he calls "trickster discourse." In his view, the trickster is "disembodied in a narrative . . . a communal sign, a comic holotrope and a discourse" ("Trickster Discourse" 196).

This rhetorical disembodiment of the trickster, however, does not drain the trickster of social or political meaning. On the contrary, as Gates and Vizenor both suggest, the trickster's linguistic operation has serious ideological implications. Gates explains that the African American signifying monkey's act of "Signifyin(g)" represents a radical undermining of the language and power structures of white America. Gates suggests that signifying amounts to a "political offensive":

> Some black genius or a community of witty and sensitive speakers emptied the signifier "signification" of its received concepts and filled this empty signifier with their own concepts. By doing so, by supplanting the received, standard English concept associated by (white) convention with this particular signifier, they (un)wittingly disrupted the nature of the sign = signified/signifier equation itself. . . . [B]y supplanting the received term's associated concept, the black vernacular tradition created a homonymic pun of the profoundest sort, thereby marking its sense of difference from the rest of the English community of speakers. Their complex act of language Signifies upon both formal language use and its conventions, conventions established, at least officially, by middle-class white people. (*Signifying* 45–46)

Thus the signifying monkey's act of "signifying" becomes a critique of "the nature of (white) meaning itself." Words such as *down, baby,* and *cool* become double-voiced, or "decolonized" by investing previously understood words with alternative and perhaps contradictory meanings (50). Gates's analysis of the signifying monkey suggests how the African American trickster becomes both a figure and a linguistic means for one culture's "guerrilla action" against its oppressing culture's language and ideology.

Gerald Vizenor similarly connects the trickster's linguistic operations to cultural politics, emphasizing the trickster's indefinability and elusiveness by associating tricksters with the slipperiness of language: "the trickster is being, nothingness and liberation; a loose seam in consciousness; that wild space over and between sounds, words, sentences and narratives" ("Trickster Discourse" 196). Yet Vizenor's postmodern view of the trickster is politically grounded: his description of trickster discourse seeks to free Native American literatures from the reductive, "tragic monologue" of cultural anthropology ("Trickster Discourse" 187). Vizenor specifically opposes his view of the trickster to a modernist view of the individualistic stoic "savage," whose survival "supported the notion of the vanishing tribes" ("Trickster Discourse" 193). Vizenor's trickster cannot be captured, precisely because he or she is not a figure but a mode of "communal signification" ("Trickster Discourse" 187). Like the signifying monkey, Vizenor's trickster discourse embodies communal and cultural strength through shared codes of meaning.[23]

In both Gates's and Vizenor's view, the trickster's postmodern operation in language signals a cultural critique of the most radical kind. The trickster's relevance to a politically revolutionary version of postmodernism has been noted by other writers as well. William Hynes notes that "the logic of order and convergence, that is logos-centrism, or logocentrism, is challenged by another path, the random and divergent trail taken by that profane metaplayer, the trickster" ("Inconclusive Conclusions" 216). Several critics connect the postmodern specifically to Americans of mixed cultural heritage, noting the usefulness of a postmodern view of identity in freeing stereotyped groups from essentializing notions of identity. "Postmodern critiques of essentialism which challenge notions of universality . . . can open up new possibilities for the construction of self," explains bell hooks (*Yearning* 28).[24] We might view the trickster, who embodies a divided, fluid, shifting identity, as a mythic trope for the postmodern. Theories of the postmodern and theories of the trickster coincide and mutually illuminate each other; perhaps trickster's biggest contribution to the postmodern is the notion that identity can be multiplicitous and that the deconstruction of a falsely unitary language need not lead to incoherence. If the tricksterized postmodernisms of Erdrich, Kingston, and Morrison are politically grounded, so too are their varieties of magical realism. Elements of the sacred, of myth and fantasy, mix with history and "fact" in their trickster novels to create an altered sense of the real that challenges perceived, western ways of knowing. Trinh T. Minh-ha notes that it is only westerners who believe that elements such as the sacred and myth are incongruous with the real. She critiques the western emphasis on clarity within a broader perspective that includes paradox: "The language of Taoism and Zen . . . which is perfectly accessible but rife with paradox does not qualify as 'clear' (paradox is 'illogical' and 'nonsensical' to many Westerners)" (16). The trickster, who embodies paradox, provides a means for Erdrich, Kingston, and Morrison to cultivate a larger sense of the real, a sense that transcends the magical realist label; the intermingling of mythic and mundane becomes another expression of a multifaceted worldview.

◎

The trickster's gift for double-voiced discourse, the ability to assume various masks and embody multiple perspectives, explains the figure's appeal in the multicultural context in which Erdrich, Kingston, and Morrison live and write. Bakhtin explains that the seeds of novel form could only have originated and flourished under conditions of "struggle between tribes, peoples, cultures and languages" such as the cultural bilingualism of ancient Rome, or, I would add, the cultural diversity of modern America (50). A decentralization of worldview depends upon an awareness of diverse social groups constantly interacting with each other. We can look at the position of Erdrich, Kingston, and Morrison in this light. Though they are not all bilingual in the traditional sense, each speaks several "languages" as they inhabit the various worlds of academia, modern popular culture, modern ethnic culture, and folk tradition.

Laguna Pueblo writer and critic Paula Gunn Allen explains of women of color that "it is not merely biculturality that forms the foundation of our lives and work . . . it is multiculturality, multilinguality, and dizzying class-crossing from the fields to the salons, from the factories to the academy, or from galleries and the groves of academe to the neighborhoods and reservations" ("'Border' Studies" 305). Similarly, in *Between Worlds*, Amy Ling notes that "the characteristics that Bakhtin identified as central to the novel in general . . . are, in particular, literally characteristic of our [Chinese American] authors. When one is not totally absorbed within a culture . . . as when one is conversant in different languages, one is able to see those cultures or languages from the outside and thus to see them more wholly than can the people imprisoned within a single language or perspective" (178). Chicana writer and critic Gloria Anzaldúa addresses this issue of language between cultures in her bilingually titled *Borderlands/La Frontera: The New Mestiza*. In her preface she describes a new "language of the borderlands" that reflects the varied "codes" of her experience—English, Castillian Spanish, Mexican Spanish, Texano, to name a few (x). Anzaldúa stresses the positive effects of this mix of languages: "At the juncture of cultures, languages cross-pollinate and are revitalized" (x).

To put it another way, because of their position "at the juncture of cultures," women writers of color are uniquely situated to speak as tricksters and to write out of a trickster aesthetic. bell hooks describes the tricksterlike "mode of seeing" that she developed as an African American growing up in a small Kentucky town:

> The railroad tracks were a daily reminder of our
> marginality. . . . Living as we did—on the edge—we
> developed a particular way of seeing reality. We looked both
> from the outside in and from the inside out. This mode of
> seeing reminded us of the existence of a whole universe, a
> main body made up of both margin and center. . . . This
> sense of wholeness, impressed upon our consciousness by the
> structure of our daily lives, provided us an oppositional world
> view—a mode of seeing unknown to most of our oppressors,
> that sustained us, aided us in our struggle to transcend
> poverty and despair, strengthened our sense of self and our
> solidarity. (*Feminist Theory* ix)

Her description recalls Turner's characterization of tricksters as "edge men" ("Myth and Symbol" 580). hooks sees this trickster positionality and its mix of subversive and affirmative survival strategies as a source of personal and communal strength.

Gloria Anzaldúa perhaps relates her sense of self to the trickster most explicitly. Recalling the trickster's place at the crossroads, she calls herself "a crossroads inhabited by whirlwinds" (*Anzaldúa and Moraga* 205). She draws on the image of the Yoruba trickster Eshu to describe the life journey of "la mestiza," the woman of mixed cultural heritage: "*Eshu, / Yoruba* god of indeterminacy, / . . . blesses her choice of path" (*Anzaldúa* 80). Anzaldúa explains that the new mestiza copes with her tricksterlike position "by developing a tolerance for contradiction, a tolerance for ambiguity. She learns to juggle cultures. She has a plural personality, she operates in a pluralistic mode. . . . Not only does she sustain contradictions, she turns the ambivalence into something else" (Anzaldúa 79). Anzaldúa's emphasis on ambivalence suggests the inability of that word, or any word, to capture her identity: "You say my name is ambivalence? Think of me as Shiva, a many-armed and legged body with one foot on brown soil, one on white, one in straight society, one in the gay world, the man's world, the women's. . . . A sort of spider woman hanging by one thin strand of web. Who me, confused? Ambivalent? Not so. Only your labels split me" (*Anzaldúa and Moraga* 205).[25] Part of the strength a trickster identity offers is its escape from the dismembering effect of affixing labels.

Paula Gunn Allen also explicitly relates women writers of color to the trickster, defining their art in specifically tricksterlike terms as "cunning crafting" and "our ways of signifyin'" ("'Border' Studies" 310, 312). The works of women of color, Allen observes, reveal the "process of living on the border, of crossing and recrossing boundaries of consciousness" ("'Border' Studies" 305). Significantly, Allen follows Henry Louis Gates Jr. in suggesting that the trickster, "who is male and female, many-tongued, changeable, changing and who contains all the meanings possible within her or his consciousness" be a model for the process of critical interpretation, a nonwestern alternative to "Eurocentric patriarchal self-preoccupation" ("'Border' Studies" 307).

Though hooks, Anzaldúa, and Allen all suggest a tricksterlike model for women writers of color, their strategic emphases are different. hooks stresses the trickster's negative task of "destroying dualism, eradicating systems of domination" (*Feminist Theory*

163), whereas Allen emphasizes the affirmative: "Artists of color can best do something other than engage in adversarial politics. . . . We need to invest our energies in our vision, our significances, and our ways of signifyin'" ("'Border' Studies" 312). Anzaldúa, perhaps truest to the trickster mode, has no one identifiable emphasis.

Drawing on this trickster positionality, Morrison, Erdrich, and Kingston become tricksters in telling their stories; they employ multiple perspectives and refuse to mediate with one clear authorial stance. By slipping in and out of different realities and states of consciousness, the writer as trickster blurs the boundaries between self and other, between male and female, between the real and the fantastic, and even between story and audience. Significantly, Morrison, Kingston, and Erdrich center their examination of sexism within their own cultures in the figure of the trickster. Battling sexism within an oppressed racial group is an especially tricky business. "When one is black," bell hooks explains, calling oneself a feminist "is likely to be heard as a devaluation of the struggle to end racism" (*Feminist Theory* 29).[26] In discussing the complex positionality of women of color, Carolyn Denard suggests a way in which many women combine a feminist with an antiracial position by espousing an "ethnic cultural feminism" that encompasses a concern with "the particular female cultural values of their own ethnic group" (171). These "female cultural values" often intersect across cultures, but because of the differing cultural histories from which they evolve, they should not be treated as identical.[27] Feminist criticism, as Hazel Carby asserts, should interrogate "sexual ideologies for their racial specificity" (18).

Tricksters in most cultures are androgynous by definition, but male tricksters are more common than female tricksters.[28] In the works of Erdrich, Kingston, and Morrison, the most prominent trickster protagonists are male: Nanapush is the trickster narrator of *Tracks*, Wittman Ah Sing is the monkey protagonist of *Tripmaster Monkey*, and Son is the modern avatar of Br'er Rabbit in *Tar Baby*. For women writers with feminist concerns, this choice seems curious, until we consider the freedom a trickster protagonist allows. Tricksters embody paradoxes, which enables them to be simultaneously heroes and scapegoats. Erdrich, Kingston, and Morrison permit the trickster to remain a symbol of cultural survival, but at the same time they explicitly question the sexism of their male tricksters, thereby critiquing the sexism of their cultures' myths and asserting counterperspectives through the novel's other voices (most notably, the narrator of *Tripmaster Monkey*, Pauline in *Tracks*, and Jadine in *Tar Baby*). Moreover, each writer values and emphasizes the trickster's androgyny, and although their most prominent tricksters are male, each revises cultural myth and folklore to create female tricksters as well: *Love Medicine*'s Lulu Lamartine, *Song of Solomon*'s Pilate, and *The Woman Warrior*'s Brave Orchid.

◎

As trickster authors, Erdrich, Kingston and Morrison revise oral traditions in written form to create their trickster aesthetic, using storytelling to shape their novels. Tricksters are consummate storytellers, wielding power over their listeners with their artful use of words. Paula Rabinowitz describes the social nature of storytelling as a narrative form: "As a social process, storytelling mediates social relations rather than providing moral prescriptions; the story's meaning is embedded in the telling, not in its final point. . . . A profoundly interactive process, storytelling provides a cultural intersection between the personal and the political, the individual and the community; the teller, the tale and the audience" (28). Trinh T. Minh-ha also emphasizes the communal and culture-building aspects of storytelling, calling it "the oldest form of building historical consciousness in community" (148). In the words of Navaho storyteller Yellowman, "Through the stories everything is made possible."[29] Stories foster and create cultural identity, connect individual listeners to a shared tradition, and reveal new possibilities.

Trickster novels use storytelling to set up dialogue among characters and with the reader, thereby lending a sense of orality to the written text. The novels' lack of closure and their privileging of differing perspectives and voices emphasize dialogue, community, and the social process of storytelling. Gerald Vizenor's description of the trickster's function in Native American oral tales illustrates the trickster's relationship to this storytelling process. The trickster's multivalence and elusiveness suggest that because no one point of view is all-encompassing, all points of view, including those of the author, the narrator, the characters, and the reader or listener, together create the meaning of a story. Vizenor sees the trickster as a "communal sign" that makes the story a communal experience by connecting the various points of view ("Trickster Discourse" 193).[30] Vizenor emphasizes the reader's crucial role in recreating the story as he or she reads: "The active reader implies the author, imagines narrative voices, inspires characters, and salutes tribal tricksters in a comic discourse" (*Trickster of Liberty* x).

Storytelling makes the reader one of the community of listeners, and trickster authors implicitly or explicitly invite and even demand reader involvement. The dialogue is not resolved in a trickster narrative, and the reader must negotiate a place within it. Leaving things open-ended or contradictory forces the reader to play a more active role in the construction of meaning, filling in the "gaps," as Wolfgang Iser says, by bringing "into play our own faculty for establishing connections" (*Implied* 280). Iser's description of the reading process in multivocal works sounds tricksterlike: "the reader's wandering viewpoint travels between all these segments, its constant switching during the timeflow of reading intertwines them, thus bringing forth a network of perspectives" ("Interaction" 113). In Vizenor's terms, the reader of a trickster narrative is acted upon as "the trickster liberates the mind" (*Trickster of Liberty* xi). The reader of trickster novels is anything but a passive, detached observer—a fact that takes on special importance in contemporary American trickster novels, which confront multicultural issues and address a multicultural audience. By becoming involved in the interpretive work, the reader becomes more sensitive to cultural boundaries and better equipped to cross them.[31] A multiplicity of voices and perspectives such as those present in a trickster novel can effect change in the reader; by engaging in dialogue with a text, readers open their own thoughts to change.[32]

The gaps that trickster authors Erdrich, Kingston, and Morrison leave in their works are sites of enormous import. As the undefined borderland between two worlds, which is the specific domain of the trickster, the gap represents both an invitation and a challenge. On the one hand, ambiguity invites unprecedented freedom of expression and interpretation, which lends to the printed words the immediacy of orality. Bonnie TuSmith explains that for Kingston ambiguity is "the creative compromise of a literate mind conveying the improvisational immediacy of oral culture" ("Literary Tricksterism" 255).[33] As Trinh T. Minh-ha vividly puts it, "Blanks, lapses, and silences . . . settle in like gaps of fresh air as soon as the inked space smells stuffy" (16).

On the other hand, although gaps allow freedom and interplay and invite reader involvement, they also challenge the reader to step into the gap rather than use the writer as an easy bridge to another culture or perspective. In "The Bridge Poem," the opening piece to *This Bridge Called My Back: Writings by Radical Women of Color*, Donna Kate Rushkin expresses the frustration and exhaustion that a trickster positionality can bring:

> I've had enough
> I'm sick of seeing and touching
> Both sides of things
> Sick of being the damn bridge for everybody
> . . . .
> I'm sick of filling in your gaps. (Anzaldúa and Moraga xxi)

She tells the reader: "Stretch or drown / Evolve or die" (Anzaldúa and Moraga xxii). Like Rushkin, all of the trickster authors in the present study demand to be met part way. Maxine Hong Kingston, for example, voices her frustrations with the "cultural mis-readings" of American reviewers of her work, finding it "sad and slow that I have to *explain*. Again. If I use my limited time and words to explain, I will never get off the ground" ("Cultural Mis-Readings" 57). Like the paradoxical trickster figure, a between-world condition "carries both negative and positive charges" and can be both exhausting and exhilarating (Ling 177). One fully belongs nowhere, yet, as Nikki Giovanni has said, "Our alienation is our great strength. Our strength is that we are not comfortable any place; therefore we're comfortable *every place.* We can go any place on earth and find a way to be comfortable" (quoted in Ling 177).[34]

In the novels of Erdrich, Kingston, and Morrison, the trickster is both "disembodied" in narrative form and a bodily presence in the novel. The trickster fuses the affirmative power of folklore with the subversive power of laughter and critique. On every level of the text, the trickster disrupts expectations, challenges the status quo, and at the same time reaffirms the values of community.

Through their "cunning crafting," Erdrich, Kingston, and Morrison create modern American tricksters, whose carnival laughter and scathing critiques challenge racial and gender stereotypes yet attest to the enduring strength of their cultural communities. These writers fulfill Shirley Geok-Lin Lim's hope for a "productive multivalence" and Gloria Anzaldúa's projection for "the new mestiza": "The future depends," Anzaldúa says, "on the straddling of two or more cultures. By creating a new mythos—that is, a change in the way we perceive reality . . . la mestiza creates a new consciousness" (Lim 32; Anzaldúa 80). Through a trickster aesthetic, the narratives of Kingston, Erdrich, and Morrison engage readers in active dialogue with the texts' multiple perspectives, engendering a broader sense of the "real" and suggesting a mode for personal and cultural survival.

◎

Though a trickster perspective is perhaps most accessible to women of color, who cross and recross gender, race, and class boundaries, Amy Ling notes that the "between world condition . . . is characteristic of all people in a minority position," including all women (177).[35] Feminist critics have suggested that a tricksterlike receptiveness to other voices, the skill of speaking in and negotiating among several languages, is characteristic of women in general. In an influential study of women's moral development, Carol Gilligan argues that women's socially learned "sensitivity to the needs of others and the assumption of responsibility for taking care lead women to attend to voices other than their own and to include in their judgment other points of view"(17). Although Gilligan's study is necessarily limited in its acknowledged disregard for historical, social, or cultural variables, it has important implications for any culture in which women are the primary caretakers. Women's sense of self, Gilligan suggests, is informed by a weblike conception of relationship; self and other are "different but connected rather than . . . separate and opposed" (147). Paula Gunn Allen seconds this view with her discussion of the "self-in-relation," asserting that "to read women's texts with any accuracy, we need a theory that places the twin concepts of I and thou securely within the interconnected matrix of all and everything" ("'Border' Studies" 314). It is important to stress that connectedness, sensitivity, and receptiveness, often assumed to be "natural" in women, are fundamentally asexual traits, which we might more appropriately associate with the trickster's androgynous openness to others.

Many critics are quick to point out the vast differences in the histories, goals, and interests of white feminists and African American, Native American, Chicana, and Asian American feminists.[36] Certainly, white American feminists have tended to ignore the lived experience of other American women in formulating their basis for protest and reform. As a white feminist critic, I have an interest in Erdrich, Morrison, and Kingston that grows out of a conviction like that of bell hooks, who states: "Every woman can stand in political opposition to sexist, racist, heterosexist, and classist oppression. . . . Women must learn to accept responsibility for fighting oppressions that may not directly affect us as individuals. . . . [The feminist movement] suffers when individual concerns and priorities are the only reason for participation. When we show our concern for the collective, we strengthen our solidarity" (*Feminist Theory* 61–62).

As the borders between cultures become paradoxically both easier to cross and more sharply delineated, tricksters will remain important figures "in the American grain" (Ellison 55). It makes sense to look to women of color, whose lives cross so many borders, for the best models of trickster strategy. In the words of Gloria Anzaldúa, "Living on borders, and in margins, keeping intact one's shifting and multiple identity and integrity, is like trying to swim in a new element. . . . There is an exhilaration in being a participant in the further evolution of humankind" (preface ix).

◎

Each of the three authors considered here centers at least one of her novels on a trickster character: Kingston's *Tripmaster Monkey*, Erdrich's *Tracks*, and Morrison's *Tar Baby*. But trickster energy inspires all of their work. Because they draw on such different traditions, I treat each author's work separately. In *The Woman War-*

rior and *China Men*, Kingston adopts the trickster as a trope for cultural exploration. *The Woman Warrior* chronicles a young girl in trickster training, learning to cope with paradox from her trickster mother, Brave Orchid, who has lived "between worlds" in both China and America. *China Men* reclaims and creates Chinese American mythic history as a chronicle of trickster ancestors, who claim America through subterfuge, alias, and revolt. Kingston's concern with the trickster culminates in *Tripmaster Monkey*, which introduces Wittman Ah Sing, Berkeley beatnik and reincarnation of the Chinese Monkey King, as a model for personal and cultural identity.

Louise Erdrich's four novels, connected by geography, history, and genealogy, invent a trickster cycle that challenges "traditional" American history and contemporary popular attitudes toward Native Americans. The evolving narrative forms of *Love Medicine*, *Tracks*, and *The Bingo Palace* express the history of a Chippewa community in trickster terms that, far from reinforcing stereotypes of a vanishing tribe, emphasize variety, vibrancy, and continuance. Erdrich creates feminist revisions of the trickster in Fleur and Lulu and, in *The Beet Queen*, critiques the fragility of trickster identity when it is not grounded in community and tradition.

Morrison's work shows a recurring preoccupation with female iconoclasts, wanderers, adventurers, and drifters. For her, the trickster offers a way to challenge traditional versions of African American female identity and imagine new alternatives. *Sula*, *Song of Solomon*, and *Tar Baby* expand on and refigure traditional African American tricksters and conjurers in ways that fundamentally question the strength of the social fabric. Whereas *Sula* exposes the challenges of a trickster positionality, *Song of Solomon*'s visionary Pilate suggests the trickster's energy and power, and *Tar Baby* presents conflicting versions of female trickster identity: tar woman Therese and unrooted, free-flying Jadine. Creator of worlds, epic bumbler, outrageous joker, expert transformer, consummate artist: the trickster lives in contemporary American literature, in all her myriad guises.

CHAPTER TWO

Monkey Business
Maxine Hong Kingston's
Transformational Trickster Texts

For upon those who live between two worlds was imposed a
spurious and in the end ignoble choice. "You must be one or
the other." Which implied a service to be performed for one or
the other representatives of a culture. I rejected this diminu-
tion of the self. . . . *I shall be both.*

Han Suyin

They would chop me up into little fragments and tag each
piece with a label. . . . Only your labels split me.

Gloria Anzaldúa

In her groundbreaking study on women writers of Chinese ancestry, *Between Worlds,* Amy Ling observes that "the feeling of being between worlds, totally at home nowhere," characterizes
writing by Chinese American women. Because of the high value
placed on feminine modesty and reticence in Chinese culture,

Ling explains, a woman of Chinese ancestry who wants to publish in the United States "must be something of a rebel, for writing, an act of rebellion and self-assertion, runs counter to Confucian training. Also she has to possess two basic character traits: an indomitable will and an unshakeable self-confidence" (14).[1] Kingston's trickster aesthetic affirms the importance of these traits in her work. The trickster Monkey, whose will, confidence, and outrageous rebellion disrupt heaven and win him battles with dragons and gods, inspires the crafting of Kingston's *Woman Warrior*, *China Men*, and *Tripmaster Monkey*. In all of her works, the trickster embodies Kingston's vision of identity and of the transformative power of narrative.

MONKEY MOTHERS AND OTHER PARADOXES: *THE WOMAN WARRIOR*

Although Kingston does not introduce an overt trickster character into her works until *Tripmaster Monkey*, the formal and thematic concerns of *The Woman Warrior* and *China Men* show signs of the trickster's influence.[2] Classified as "autobiography," and labeled as nonfiction on its cover, *The Woman Warrior* transgresses both of these restrictive definitions and offers a trickster-inspired model for narrative form and the construction of identity. As a trickster text, *The Woman Warrior* encourages a sense of truth as multifaceted, both through the example of the trickster mother, Brave Orchid, and through a narrative that demands and plays on reader involvement.

Though much of the criticism of *The Woman Warrior* focuses on the difficulties created by competing and often contradictory allegiances,[3] such contradiction is not necessarily debilitating.

Kingston's multivocal *Woman Warrior* redefines *autobiography* as a process of acknowledging and giving voice to contradictions and paradoxes within the self. The trickster, whose identity is not stable but always shifting, who speaks in many languages and challenges preconceived notions, embodies this process. The trickster's androgynous, multivocal, polyvalent identity reconciles or encompasses the "agonizing contradictions" that split women writers by their allegiance to various groups (Hunt 11). Like Han Suyin's avowal that "I shall be both" and Gloria Anzaldúa's assertion that "only your labels split me," Kingston's autobiography affirms a fluid, tricksterlike identity not bounded by restrictive definitions (Ling 115; Anzaldúa and Moraga 205).[4] Kingston's conception of identity in *The Woman Warrior* challenges a predominantly male tradition in Asian American literature, which stresses a monolithic, unified identity.[5] Robert Lee connects the form of the work to a political subversion of the status quo, suggesting one way in which *The Woman Warrior* plays a trickster role in relation to Asian American tradition: "It is precisely the discontinuities, dislocations, and erasures in the history of Chinese women in the United States that *The Woman Warrior* interrogates, thereby challenging both the silence imposed by Orientalism and the authoritarianism of a reasserted patriarchy that threatens to seal Chinese American women's experiences off in its masculinized revision of history" (55). In the spirit of the trickster, *The Woman Warrior* outrageously pokes holes in stereotypes and established hierarchies. The text uses trickster strategies both to challenge a stultifying patriarchy and to champion an ethnic Chinese American culture that, in the face of harsh discriminatory laws, has had to rely on trickster strategies for its continuity. It is "camouflage, subterfuge and surprise that enable the immigrant traditions to survive and [that] imbue them with power for resistance" (Lee 57).

Kingston's autobiography incorporates memoir, novel, myth, fantasy, legend, and biography and thus not only challenges an Asian American male tradition but also rejects a view of the self as an isolated individual. The author's remark that "I hope my writing has many layers, as human beings have layers," encourages us to read the self as composed of multiple stories ("Cultural Mis-Readings" 65). *The Woman Warrior* encompasses the voices and perspectives of the narrator's mother, her aunts, her sister, and her grandmother, as well as mythical forebears Fa Mu Lan and Ts'ai Yen, and thereby suggests a notion of identity that includes one's community and culture.[6] "'I' am nothing but who 'I' am in relation to other people," Kingston explains ("Personal Statement" 23). This relational view of identity calls for a fluid conception of autobiography as a form that creates and preserves community as well as individuality. She feels compelled to invent a new autobiographical form, she explains, because "we're always on the brink of disappearing. Our culture's disappearing and our communities are always disappearing" (Fishkin 786). Kingston's autobiography gives voice to the many women who have created community for her.

As a gathering of varied and often contradictory stories, *The Woman Warrior* explores a sense of truth that allows for paradox. The tricksterlike image of the elusive, ever-changing dragon appears throughout *The Woman Warrior*, suggesting the impossibility of a single all-encompassing perspective. The narrator, as Fa Mu Lan, learns about paradox through dragons: "I learned to make my mind large, as the universe is large, so that there is room for paradoxes. . . . The dragon lives in the sky, ocean, marshes, and mountains; and the mountains are also its cranium. Its voice thunders and jingles like copper pans. It breathes fire and water; and sometimes the dragon is one, sometimes many" (*WW* 29).[7] Like truth, the dragon can never be seen in its entirety and therefore forms a central trope in the text for the indeterminacy of any one point of view.[8] The idea that paradox may be the most accurate representation of truth becomes clear when the narrator speculates about her mother cutting her frenum. "She pushed my tongue up and sliced the frenum. Or maybe she snipped it with a pair of scissors. I don't remember her doing it. . . . I saw no scars in my mouth." The narrator is unsure not only about how but also whether and why her mother cut her frenum: "Sometimes I felt very proud that my mother committed such a powerful act upon me. At other times I was terrified—the first thing my mother did when she saw me was to cut my tongue." In the same act, the mother silences her daughter and frees her tongue "to move in any language" (*WW* 164). The passage captures the ambivalence of the narrator's relationship to her mother and the paradoxically debilitating and empowering effect Brave Orchid has on her.

As Brave Orchid teaches her daughter to value paradox, she passes on a trickster legacy, for Brave Orchid, whose very name is a paradox, is a trickster who undermines and upsets the injunctions that she delivers. The mother's legacy to her daughter is necessarily complex because she represents for her daughter the oppressive authority of Chinese culture, especially regarding acceptable female behavior. Yet through her actions and her stories, Brave Orchid sends vivid messages that subvert her authoritarian proclamations. The no name aunt's story dramatizes this tension between an oppressive overt message—"Don't humiliate us" (*WW* 5)—and a subtle message of rebellion; like the narrator, who flouts her mother's injunction not to tell, Brave Orchid herself has broken a taboo by telling the story of the no name aunt to her daughter. Though "You must not tell" carries the force of command, Brave Orchid's later request, "Don't let your father know that I told you," betrays her own sense of transgression and sets up a clandestine alliance with her daughter against the father (*WW* 5). Brave Orchid hands down a secret legacy of powerful stories to her daughter, who muses, "I have believed that . . . words [were] so strong and fathers so frail that 'aunt' would do my father some mysterious harm" (*WW* 15).

Contradiction and paradox, the trickster's hallmarks, define Brave Orchid. She slyly communicates trickster strategies to her daughter through the disparity between her words and her actions. Though she openly repeats misogynistic sayings like "'There's no profit in raising girls. Better to raise geese than girls,'" Brave Orchid sings the legend of Fa Mu Lan to her daughter, thereby giving her a means to fight against tradition. "She said I would grow up a wife and a slave, but she taught me the song of the warrior woman" (*WW* 20). Brave Orchid's life story, told in "Shaman," suggests that her example as a deserted wife turned doctor, who would cross the ocean to bear six children after the age of forty-five, provides another powerful antidote to her misogynist maxims.

As the protagonist struggles to come to terms with her cultural heritage, she must wrestle with her mother's confusing, contradictory, cryptic stories (*WW* 163). "'I don't want to listen to any more of your stories; they have no logic. They scramble me up. You lie with stories. You won't tell me a story and then say, "This is a true story," or "This is just a story." . . . I can't tell what's real and what you make up'" (*WW* 202). The book records the process of the narrator's gradual acceptance that truth is multi-faceted. Reality encompasses different, sometimes conflicting versions, and the enigmatic Brave Orchid, both woman and shaman, has trickily equipped not crippled her daughter by conveying this. Whereas the naive protagonist struggles with distinctions between "a true story" and "just a story," the narrator finally collapses these distinctions by presenting herself as a tricksterlike "outlaw knotmaker" whose story is a mix of actual, fictional, and mythic events (*WW* 163).

As *The Woman Warrior* works to subvert the protagonist's polarized thinking, it does the same for the reader. The narration of Moon Orchid's adventures in "At the Western Palace" provides a useful example of how the text questions the relative values of "a true story" and "just a story." Kingston will not allow her reader to rest comfortably with the separation of "fiction" and "fact," or with the idea that either possesses a higher claim to reality. "At the Western Palace," the fourth section of *The Woman Warrior*, is an extended third-person omniscient narrative, thoroughly grounded in the mundane details of modern life. With its classic short story structure, the chapter seems at first glance to be the most "realistic" and accessible and therefore the most reliable of the work's five sections.[9] However, the opening words of the next section destabilize that comfortable trust in the narrator's omniscience: "What my brother actually said was" (*WW* 164). Not having witnessed most of the events herself, Kingston has embellished her brother's version of the story. She considers the relative worth of the two stories and concedes, "His version of the story may be better than mine because of its bareness, not twisted into designs" (*WW* 164). Yet although she suggests that her brother's story may be closer to the "facts," her inclusion of "At the Western Palace" implies that she is proud of her outlaw knotmaking. Indeed, although the brother drove Brave Orchid and her sister to Los Angeles and participated in some of the story's events, he is limited by his perspective. His brief statements highlight his absorption in his own role: "I drove Mom and Second Aunt to Los Angeles to see Aunt's husband who's got the other wife. . . . I don't remember [what Mom said]. I pretended a pedestrian broke her leg so he would come" (*WW* 163). The narrator's fictionalized version of the story, which imaginatively enters the minds of the participants ("Moon Orchid was so ashamed, she held her hands over her face. She wished she could also hide her dappled hands" [*WW* 153]), may be truer than a firsthand account.

In presenting alternative variations on stories, Kingston's tricksterlike narrative acts upon her reader in much the same way as Brave Orchid's stories act upon the narrator. Vicente Gotera records student responses to *The Woman Warrior* that sound much like Kingston's narrator: "I had trouble determining whether a particular storyline was truth or fantasy," one student writes (65).[10] Like Brave Orchid's story of the no name aunt, Kingston tells us "once and for all the useful parts" (*WW* 6), leaving gaps and blanks in her story that test the reader's "strength to establish realities" (*WW* 5). Kingston explains, "I meant to give people those questions so that they can wrestle with them in their own lives. You know, I can answer those questions, but then . . . I just answer [them] for me. . . . When people wrestle with them and struggle with them in their own minds and in their own lives, all kinds of exciting things happen to them" (Fishkin 785). Kingston implies that there is no definitive way to fill the gaps in the text—the answers to the questions that the text raises change according to the reader. Kingston's comments suggest that she sees reading as an interactive process. When readers encounter a trickster text, "all kinds of exciting things happen to them," as they, like Kingston's narrator, wrestle with unresolved contradictions and perhaps begin to question their own comfortable way of viewing the world.

TRICKSTER HISTORY: *CHINA MEN*

If *The Woman Warrior*'s narrator is a trickster-in-training who grows up learning to distrust received truths, *China Men*'s narrator steps even further outside of her own point of view to tell the fathers' stories.[11] *China Men* combines history, biography, autobiography, myth, fiction, and fantasy to reclaim and recreate Chinese American history as a multilayered story. "What I am doing is putting many kinds of stories and people right next to one another, as they are in real life. Each character is viewed from the vantage point of the others" (Pfaff 26). The work celebrates Kingston's ancestors, and by extension all China men, as tricksters who survived and triumphed despite unjust immigration laws and labor practices.

Like *The Woman Warrior*, *China Men* has proved a difficult work to classify under traditional genre categories. Primarily viewed as "biography" or "history," it also contains autobiographical vignettes, western and Chinese myths and legends, and multiple versions of a single life. If *The Woman Warrior*'s structure reflects a multilayered self, *China Men*'s structure reflects a multilayered community, culture, and history. To truly tell the story of China men, Kingston creates a communal chronicle, which reminds us that history is composed of many lives and many stories—not *his* story but *their* stories. She includes an eight-page section composed of U.S. immigration laws, which she calls "pure history," in order to combat mainstream readers' ignorance of the Chinese American immigrant experience, but the section's dry, official tone emphasizes the limitations of the history genre (Pfaff 25). The collective mode of *China Men* subverts a traditional, monologic history that—as Kingston's need to include "The Laws" implies—has all but erased Chinese Americans (Goellnicht 196).

In addition to challenging conventional written history, Kingston's work fights to recover an oral legacy that she senses has already been lost. Unlike Kingston's mother, who passes on a rich oral tradition to her daughter, her father remains silent, and she must invent his stories herself. *China Men* is Kingston's talk-story to her father: "I'll tell you what I suppose from your silences and a few words, and you can tell me that I'm mistaken. You'll just have to speak up with the real stories if I've got you wrong" (*CM* 15).[12] This narrative stance recalls trickster Nanapush's direct address to Lulu in Louise Erdrich's *Tracks*, but here the roles are reversed: rather than a grandfather passing down an oral legacy to his granddaughter, here the daughter must reimagine her father's and grandfathers' stories, underscoring the precariousness of the oral tradition.

That Kingston had to separate the stories of her family into two volumes to reflect the historical and geographic split between Chinese American men's and women's experiences accounts in part for the breach in the oral tradition from father to daughter. Additionally, one incident in *China Men* suggests that Kingston's own fear and resentment of her male relatives' misogyny has prevented her from hearing the men's stories in the past. It involves Kau Goong, her grandmother's adventurous brother: "My brothers remember him as a generous old man; he took them to a smoking place where men with silver and wood pipes gave them presents and praised them. The only times he spoke to me were to scold and to give orders. 'Bad girl,' he said" (*CM* 180).[13] When Kau Goong comes in the house looking for her one day, his loud shouts send her scurrying to the cellar to avoid "his bossy presence" (*CM* 180). Though she successfully avoids a confrontation that day, years later at his funeral she muses, "I listened to find out more about Kau Goong's pillages, his plunders, and sackings . . . but they did not mention his crimes though he was safe from deportation now. I should have yelled questions at him. I shouldn't have hidden from him" (*CM* 185). Kingston imaginatively retells the stories of China men to recover a history silenced by missed communication. As the Kau Goong episode ironically implies, patriarchal misogyny has nearly extinguished this heroic tradition by squelching the female voice that can pass it on.

China Men's introductory chapter, "On Discovery," foregrounds issues of gender and discovery by adapting an incident from the eighteenth-century Chinese novel *Flowers in the Mirror*.[14] The segment demonstrates Kingston's trickster techniques: adaptation, invention, and defamiliarization. In Kingston's version, Tang Ao, a male scholar and traveler, "discovers" the "Land of Women" and is forced to endure the pain and humiliation of becoming a traditional female courtesan, with bound feet, plucked brows, pierced ears, and painted face. Though Kingston preserves the essential details of the eighteenth-century story

(Cheung, *Articulate* 102), she switches some characters (in the original version the tortures are inflicted on Tang Ao's brother-in-law) and relocates the Land of Women to North America. Several critics have noted the double-edged commentary Kingston's transposition of this story allows, as both a sympathetic allegory for the emasculation of Chinese men in America and (as in the original version) a critique of patriarchy that has subjected Chinese women to similar treatment for centuries.[15]

Kingston's prominent placement of the Tang Ao myth in a chapter titled "On Discovery" in a book that questions the monologic voice of history raises crucial questions about the nature of historic discoveries. Traditional myths of American history begin with its "discovery" by Christopher Columbus. Kingston's adaptation ends by suggesting that the Land of Women (or North America) was discovered by the Chinese as early as A.D. 441 (*CM* 5). This casually mentioned "fact" challenges the legitimacy and primacy of western myths of discovery by predating them and claiming the discovery of America for the Chinese, but it also questions the motives of such discovery. *Discovery* is a primary imperialist euphemism, designed to obscure the issue of prior inhabitancy in order to appropriate land for one's own purposes. When Tang Ao "discovers" the Land of Women, he remains unthreatened even though they immediately capture him: "if he had had male companions, he would've winked over his shoulder" (*CM* 3). As Tang Ao's fate makes abundantly clear, discovery does not equal possession; in fact, Tang Ao's ignorance of the civilization he "discovers" and his entrapment in his own sexist ideas of women prevent him from seeing them as potentially dangerous and result in his becoming *their* possession.[16] By destabilizing the term *discovery*, Kingston prepares readers to consider the alternative viewpoints and potential threats that lie behind their unexamined preconceptions.

Kingston not only relocates Chinese stories in North America but also recasts western myths as Chinese tales, most notably pirating Daniel Defoe's enormously popular novel *Robinson Crusoe* as "The Adventures of Lo Bun Sun." As David Leiwei Li has observed, Kingston faithfully preserves the original story, changing only outward details such as Lo Bun Sun's cultivation of rice ("American Canon" 489). The effects of this transformation are manifold. Defamiliarizing the story forces readers to consider the assumptions underlying this master narrative of western imperialism. Kingston's adaptation reveals Crusoe's justification as "one of protocolonizer, imposer of Western norms. . . . Kingston's creative reproduction of the Robinson myth lays bare the device that rationalizes almost all Western colonization, the workings of language and culture that presuppose the inherent supremacy of European civilization and the barbarous wretchedness of the native" (Li, "American Canon" 489). Exposing the motives of Robinson Crusoe (and by extension western colonization) through parody is a primary trickster strategy. As in *The Woman Warrior*, where Brave Orchid's view of all whites as ghosts and Moon Orchid's view of America as a "wilderness" of barbarians speak for Kingston's view of ethnocentrism as a human tendency not limited to westerners (*WW* 158), Kingston wields her trickster critique of ethnocentrism in *China Men*. By so easily recasting Defoe's tale as the story of a Chinese "Lo Bun Sun," Kingston shows that racism and ethnocentrism are not exclusively western but are fundamentally human foibles. Thus, like the double-edged Tang Ao myth that cuts at both racist treatment of China men in America and sexist treatment of women in China, Kingston's "Adventures of Lo Bun

Sun" parodies the myth of European supremacy while hinting that such blind self-aggrandizement is not exclusive to the western world.

The lives and stories of men of Chinese ancestry in America might easily lend themselves to tragic forms: exploited workers, unwilling bachelors, mocked and degraded "Chinamen" in a racist society. Yet rather than suggesting a history of victimization, Kingston presents the stories of her fathers and grandfathers in a comic mode. They are dauntless, irrepressible tricksters, outwitting a system stacked against them. King-Kok Cheung describes the trickster spirit that pervades *China Men:* "A subversive imagination and a sense of play enable both the dispossessed natives and the exploited Chinese immigrants to survive despite the odds. The author's own transformation of tragedy into comedy exemplifies the characteristics she attributes to China Men and engages the reader in a way no straight-faced account of peonage could" (*Articulate* 105). With her own "subversive imagination," Kingston has clearly inherited her trickster sensibility from a long line of trickster ancestors, female and male.

Kingston's father emerges as trickster in *China Men* in the sheer multiplicity of his life stories. "In the course of the book, I have him coming into this country in five different ways. I'm very proud of that," Kingston comments (Pfaff 26). The early chapter "On Fathers" radically questions a child's ability to know her parent at all. One evening she and her siblings, waiting at the gate for their father to come home, think they see him coming and run to greet him, only to be told that they are mistaken. "Looking closely, we saw that he probably was not [our father]," Kingston remembers. The man walks away, looking "from the back, almost exactly" like their father, and moments later their own father appears and acknowledges them. Placed prominently as *China Men*'s second chapter and appearing before any stories of real fathers and grandfathers, "On Fathers" destabilizes the notion of "father" as a fixed, recognizable identity. That his children look to recognize him by his expensive suit and wingtip shoes, and so easily mistake him for someone else, suggests how little they know of the man inside. In a way, both men in this incident are Kingston's father: the one who denies her and walks away and the one who salutes her.

The two chapters dedicated to her father's life, "The Father from China" and "The American Father," presented as if they concerned different people, reflect the father's multiple identities. Both chapters present him as a man of resilience and invention. Despite Kingston's ambivalence toward his misogyny and stony silence, her portrayal of her father as a heroic trickster speaks for her admiration of him. Like the Chinese trickster Monkey, he studies rigorously for years, successfully passes his examinations (Monkey's earn him the knowledge of immortality), grows dissatisfied with the mediocrity and bureaucracy that surround him, and makes his own "Journey to the West."[17] In America the father renames himself Edison, claiming for himself the cunning and resourcefulness of the famous inventor. After being duped out of the laundry business by his friends in New York, dodging arrest as manager of a gambling house, and enduring a depression that keeps him rooted to his chair as immovably as Monkey trapped for five hundred years under a mountain, Ed springs back to life and builds a new laundry in California, a self-made man many times over.

Kingston's other male ancestors are also heroic tricksters. Kingston's "crazy" grandfather, Ah Goong, shares the trickster's traditional position at the bottom of the social ladder, scorned by a family who calls him "Fleaman" and disregarded as crazy by many of his fellow railroad workers.[18] Filled with the trickster's comic and arrogant sexuality, aloft in a basket blasting into the side of a cliff, Ah Goong shouts "I am fucking the world" (*CM* 133). Though discredited as crazy, Ah Goong wisely recognizes that his work on the railroad makes him an American. He tells the men who die building the railroad, "This is the Gold Mountain. We're marking the land now. The track sections are numbered, and your family will know where we leave you" (*CM* 138). Ah Goong helps organize the railroad workers, passing along the encoded message to strike by tying holiday food bundles with a "special pattern of red string" (*CM* 140). Kingston uses Ah Goong to subtly challenge stereotyped images of Chinese men and replace them with images of strength and heroism: "Ah Goong acquired another idea that added to his reputation for craziness: The pale, thin Chinese scholars and the rich men fat like Buddhas were less beautiful, less manly than these brown muscular railroad men, of whom he was one. One of ten thousand heroes" (*CM* 142). With their strike, Ah Goong and his compatriots overturn the oppressive power structure, demanding and securing a measure of freedom and respect.

Bak Goong, the "Great Grandfather of the Sandalwood Mountains," is also a trickster.[19] He fights a no-talking rule at the Hawaiian labor camp by singing subversive messages to his compatriots, a trickster technique often used by African American slaves. After he is whipped for singing, he eventually finds his solution in the less articulate but equally effective technique of coughing out his thoughts. Like Nanapush of Erdrich's *Tracks*,

Bak Goong soon discovers that his life depends on talking. He becomes the camp storyteller, a "talk addict" who inspires the men with stories of trickster Chan Moong Gut. During one comic episode, Bak Goong and his friends mock female missionaries, making lewd comments in a dialect they don't understand and offering them more and more tea to force them to urinate.[20] Later, Bak Goong explains to the men that they have reenacted a trickster story, "Chan Moong Gut and the Gambling Wives," which connects them to a comic, subversive trickster tradition. In a hilarious defamiliarization of one of western culture's most sacred images, Bak Goong observes the "Jesus demonesses" hand out "grisly cards with a demon nailed to a cross, probably a warning about what happened to you if you didn't convert" (*CM* 112).

When Bak Goong becomes ill, he attributes it to pent-up speech: "His tongue was heavy and his throat blocked. He awoke certain that he had to cure himself by talking whenever he pleased. . . . 'Uncles and Brothers, I have diagnosed our illness. It is a congestion from not talking. What we have to do is talk and talk'" (*CM* 115). He then tells them a story that "cannot be left unsaid," about a king who relieves himself by shouting his secret into the ground (*CM* 116).[21] The story inspires the men to dig an "ear into the world," into which they shout all their secrets, frustrations, joys, and sorrows (*CM* 117). A trickster who invents and creates culture, Bak Goong tells the men, "That wasn't a custom. We made it up. We can make up customs because we're the founding ancestors of this place" (*CM* 117). Their new custom has the positive effects of a trickster strategy: their show of anger, rage, despair, and joy wins them more freedom and independence from the intimidated whites.

Like Bak Goong's shouting party, Kingston's art is collabora-
tive, and it simultaneously expresses rage at her forefathers' mis-
treatment and joy at their victories. One of the few women's stories recounted in *China Men*—the singing and crying ritual
performed before her mother's wedding—perhaps best captures
the novel's trickster spirit. Since the trickster opposes entrenched
oppression of all kinds, it is not surprising to find feminist critique alongside tribute to male ancestors. The women gather to
listen to the bride's lament, a litany of anger, sorrow, and hope at
the prospect of a new life with her husband and his family: "The
women punctuated her long complaints with clangs of pot lids
for cymbals. The rhymes made them laugh. MaMa wailed, her
eyes wet, and sang as she laughed and cried, mourned, joked,
praised, found the appropriate old songs and invented new songs
in melismata of singing and keening. She sang for three evenings.
The length of her laments that ended in sobs and laughter was
wonderful to hear" (*CM* 31). Balancing sobs and laughter, finding appropriate old songs and inventing new ones, Kingston's
China Men continues this dynamic, self-renewing, trickster-
inspired tradition.

THE MONKEY AND HIS COMMUNITY: *TRIPMASTER MONKEY*

Whereas *The Woman Warrior* and *China Men* employ trickster
strategies in themes and form—challenging genre labels, evoking a paradox-rich reality, tricking and teaching with numerous
story versions—Kingston's 1989 novel, *Tripmaster Monkey*, confirms the centrality of the trickster to Kingston's work, not only
by employing a trickster aesthetic formally but also by introduc-

ing a trickster protagonist as a model for personal and cultural identity. A full-blown trickster novel, *Tripmaster Monkey* is a groundbreaking, boundary-breaking work that revises and reinvents cultural myths, resists conventional plotting, and unsettles the reader's comfortable assumptions. The novel's protagonist, Wittman Ah Sing, is a Berkeley beatnik and modern American incarnation of the Monkey King of Chinese legend, whose adventures were crystallized in Wu Ch'eng-en's sixteenth-century novel, *Journey to the West.* Monkey attains immortality through his perseverance and audacity and repeatedly disrupts bureaucratic order in Heaven and on earth until he finally embarks upon a journey to bring the Buddhist Scriptures to China from India. Thus he combines temerity with grace and commands our laughter and our respect.

Wandering in and around San Francisco, negotiating cultural borderlines, crusading against racism and questioning the American dream, Wittman interweaves Chinese mythic history and American Romantic values as he works out his identity as a Chinese American man. Wittman's wanderings culminate in his final creation, a "combination revue-lecture" designed, Kingston tells us, to "entertain and educate the solitaries which make up a community" (*TM* 288). A metaphor for the novel's storytelling process, the play's multiple-voiced presentation and culturally mixed audience constitute Kingston's vision of communal unity in storytelling. As both clown and savior, Wittman the Monkey trickster gathers a new American community to participate in his play, which wages a war against racism and celebrates the community as a place of healing.

Wittman's scars from racism are deep: on the first page of *Tripmaster Monkey* he contemplates suicide. While he fights against the alienation, racism, and stereotyping he finds both within himself and in others, he creates an identity of interwoven cultural strands. Kingston emphasizes the worldwide roots of Wittman's identity with her encyclopedic allusions. An English major at Berkeley in the sixties, Wittman is steeped in Shakespeare, Rilke, Woolf, Beckett, Whitman, Thoreau, Ginsberg, Kerouac, and countless others, as well as in American popular culture and the Chinese classic novels *The Water Margin*, *Journey to the West*, and *Romance of the Three Kingdoms*. Like the quintessentially American poet for whom he is named, Wittman celebrates the diversity of America and strives for integration of himself and the world in the face of racism and a disintegrating community. Kingston comments in an interview that Wittman sees integration "on simple levels, such as integrating the busses and the bathrooms. . . . But he also has to work on integrating himself. And then there's that large integration between him and the rest of the universe. And America" (M. Chin 60). To Kingston, "integration" does not mean melting down differences, but harmonizing diverse and conflicting elements, whether within the self or in a larger community. The monkey trickster, "man of a thousand faces," master of seventy-two transformations, is an ideal trope for an integrated selfhood (*TM* 25).

As a monkey, Wittman remains always on the radical fringe even while he galvanizes the community to action. His long hair, beard, and eccentric clothes signal his defiance of communal norms: "people who wear black turtleneck sweaters have no place. You don't easily come home, come back to Chinatown, where they give you the stink-eye and call you a saang-hsu lo, a whisker-growing man, Beatnik" (*TM* 11). Wittman exists on the margins

not only of Chinatown but also of an explicitly American consumer culture; he dresses in shoes left on beaches and ties found
on trees, decorates his room from India Imports garbage dump-
sters, and eats the last piece of pizza others leave behind. Combining the legacy of Benjamin Franklin with that of the trickster,
he declares himself "self-made . . . out of dregs and slags" (*TM*
207). Wittman announces his own mythic status in American su-
perhero terms: "Listen, Lois," he says to Nanci, "underneath
these glasses . . . I am really: the present-day U.S.A. incarnation
of the King of the Monkeys" (*TM* 33). The pairing of Superman
and Monkey signals Wittman's dual cultural inheritance yet emphasizes his Americanness. By allowing Wittman to be both
mythic and realistic, Kingston treads a thin line between fantasy
and reality in *Tripmaster Monkey*, much as she does in *The Woman
Warrior.* Wittman himself insists on the reality of his mythic identity: "Not 'supposed to be.' I *am*" a monkey, he says to Taña (*TM*
191). As an American Monkey, Wittman uses his "Monkey
powers—outrage and jokes" to "spook out prejudice," bust through
stereotypes, and finally, create a community (*TM* 241, 332).

Because his culture is, in Kingston's words, "on the brink of
disappearing," Wittman's search for identity ultimately involves
recreating his community (Fishkin 786). The new community he
envisions consists not only of other American-born Chinese
Americans but also of everyone he meets: "Do the right thing by
whoever crosses your path," he decides. "Those coincidental
people are your people" (*TM* 223). This is why he searches out
PoPo, the mysterious pseudo-grandmother who arrived one day
on his parents' doorsteps and whom his parents finally abandon
in the mountains when she becomes a burden to them. Although

Wittman never determines the truth of his blood relationship to PoPo, the mystery is ultimately irrelevant; she is his relative if only by virtue of coincidence. PoPo's abandonment signals the breakdown of the community that Wittman must rebuild, mainly through an accretion of stories.

Communities survive by their stories, and tricksters are consummate storytellers. "Got no money. Got no home. Got story," Wittman says (*TM* 175). Wittman uses stories to preserve and renew his Chinese American culture and community, persuading an old man at the Benevolent Association to let him stage his play by enacting a Monkey episode from *Journey to the West*. His story secures a stage for the building of community. In addition to being a plot device that moves the action of the novel forward, storytelling forms the substance of the narrative itself. In picaresque trickster fashion, the novel resists linear development with its loose anecdotal construction and frequent talk-story forays. The reader must give up a search for plot in a narration whose very substance is interruptions, sidetrips, and verbal fireworks to be enjoyed for their own sake, even as their abundance threatens to overshadow those who relay them. The novel's narrator teases the reader about the trappings of traditional plotting and calls attention to its artificiality. "If there is a plot to life, then his setting out in search of her will cause PoPo to appear" (*TM* 207). Rather than finding her when he sets out on his quest, Wittman runs into PoPo anticlimactically, on the street while doing his laundry. Like Wittman, who is writing a "play that continues like life," with *Tripmaster Monkey* Kingston appears to be deliberately writing an antifiction, flaunting her own ability to invent or not invent an exciting moment in order to render life more truthfully (*TM* 169).

Critics have noted the postmodern quality of Kingston's writing.[22] Pointing to the novel's "disjunctured, decentralized perspective," Patricia Lin describes *Tripmaster Monkey*'s narrative structure as a "pastiche" of "pre-scripted texts" that Wittman gathers because "there are no new stories" (Lin 337). Though *Tripmaster Monkey* does indeed share many important aspects of postmodernism, its focus on a culturally based trickster injects a positive sense of exuberance, enthusiasm, and possibility into Kingston's writing that contradicts the ennui characteristic of much postmodern writing. Rather than producing a sense of incoherence or meaninglessness, Kingston's pastiche can be read as multivocality, designed to evoke the richness of a diverse culture. The multiple and conflicting voices in *Tripmaster Monkey*, as well as its borrowings from sources such as Rilke, *Journey to the West*, Chang and Eng, American movies, and Beat generation poetry, define the diverse cultural milieu against which and out of which Wittman must create an identity and forge a community.

Wittman's, and Kingston's, cultural inheritance is both eastern and western. In fact, as "postmodern" as Kingston's narrative technique is, it also shares many of the aspects of traditional Chinese novels. As C. T. Hsia explains, because classic Chinese novels evolved in part from a tradition of oral storytellers, who would parcel out the story in sessions at a tea house for a year or more, the narratives tend to be rambling, lengthy, and episodic. Hsia's description of these narratives is strikingly reminiscent of *Tripmaster Monkey:* "In such elaborate retelling, the plot as such becomes almost irrelevant; at each session the storyteller attends to a fraction of an episode with vivid impersonations of characters and free-ranging comments on manners and morals" (Hsia 9). Hsia's assessment of *Journey to the West*, that it is too long and repetitive though "invariably narrated with gusto," echoes many readers' reactions to *Tripmaster Monkey* (Hsia 113).[23]

Tripmaster Monkey is multivocal not only in its extensive use of other texts but also in its exploration of the heteroglossia of contemporary American life. In order to describe Wittman's experience adequately, the novel creates an American vernacular language that mixes elements of various social worlds in which Wittman moves. Kingston's use of idiomatic, spoken American language captures the tones of a broad range of diverse social groups—from tripping "hippy-dippies" to slick retail advertising campaigns, from his mother's swift, clacking mah-jongg table to his father's gruff poker group, from Mrs. Chew's warnings about "molly-see-no cherries" to the bureaucratic platitudes of the Unemployment Office. Kingston's interest in inventing a new American language places her, as she puts it, "in the tradition of American writers who consciously set out to create the literature of a new culture. Mark Twain, Walt Whitman, Gertrude Stein, the Beats all developed an ear for dialect, street language" (Li, "American Canon" 496). In Bakhtinian terms, a new language means a new worldview. Wittman's search for a new language connects language with social force and ultimately with the possibility of social change. "Where's our ain't-taking-no-shit-from-nobody street-strutting language?" Wittman asks, adding, "I want so bad to be the first bad-jazz China Man bluesman of America" (*TM* 27). Nanci's reaction to Wittman's poetry, "you sound black," is upsetting to him primarily because it suggests imitation rather than invention (*TM* 32). For an ethnic group often stereotyped as quiet and polite, it is especially important, Wittman feels, to generate a bold, creative, distinctive voice. Wittman's movement from poetry to theatrical performance significantly relates to defining an ethnic identity; because his appearance, unlike his poetic voice, cannot be mistaken as "black," when Wittman appears in the theater his difference gains center stage.

MONKEY BUSINESS: REVISIONIST MYTHMAKING

Kingston's focus on creating the language of a new culture involves inventing new stories, contributing to what she calls an "ever-changing mythology" that evolves from a vast array of cultural sources (Li, "American Canon" 496). Aware of the dangers of pastiche, *Tripmaster*'s narrator warns that "Wittman, the fool for books, ought to swear off reading for a while, and find his own life" (*TM* 168). Creating new American stories is sometimes a struggle for Wittman, as Kingston's juxtaposition of new and old stories suggests. After staying up all night inventing adventures as a traveling storyboatman in China, Wittman wakes up to realize that "he had been tripping out on the wrong side of the street. The wrong side of the world. What had he to do with foreigners? With F.O.B. [Fresh-Off-the-Boat] emigres? Fifth generation native Californian that he was. . . . His province is America" (*TM* 41). The narrative is interrupted at this point with an episode from *Journey to the West*, which both offers an implicit interpretation of the story itself and illuminates Wittman's difficulties:

> It's all right. Wittman was working out what this means:
> After a thousand days of quest . . . Monkey and his friends,
> Tripitaka on the white horse, Piggy, and Mr. Sandman, arrive
> in the West. The Indians give them scrolls, which they load

on the white horse. Partway home, Monkey, a suspicious
fellow, unrolls the scrolls, and finds that they are blank scrolls.
"What's this? We've been cheated. Those pig-catchers gave
us nothing. Let's demand an exchange.' So, he and his
companions go back, and they get words, including the
Heart Sutra. But the empty scrolls had been the right ones
all along. (*TM* 42)

Kingston's interjection of this story at a moment of crisis in
Wittman's identity as a writer suggests parallels between
Wittman's quest for the right subject and Monkey's quest for the
sacred scrolls. Wittman, like Monkey, mistrusts blank scrolls, stories yet unwritten. But because he has arrived in America, another "West," the blank ones are the right ones: Wittman lives in
a new place that demands new writing.

Part of that new writing involves updating and changing classic stories to explore contemporary American issues. In *Tripmaster Monkey* as in *The Woman Warrior,* Kingston engages in tricksterlike revisionist mythmaking, and in the process she invents
"new archetypes" for contemporary America (Fishkin 783).
Kingston's revisionist aims in *Tripmaster Monkey* are threefold:
first, she writes new versions of classic Chinese novels to create
new, alternative visions of identity and community; second,
through Wittman, she examines contemporary cultural myths to
critique harmful stereotypes and negative representations of
Chinese Americans; and finally, taking her cue from the talk-
story of a movie, she invents a new kind of art to reflect her alternative vision.

Several critics have noted Kingston's use of classic Chinese
novels, but interestingly, each focuses on a different root novel.[24]

In fact, Kingston liberally includes elements of *Journey to the West*, *Romance of the Three Kingdoms*, and *The Water Margin*. Each critic's identification of a single source stems perhaps from a desire to simplify a dizzying display of myth or to single out a specific thematic thread. However, Wittman's play cannot be pinned to one particular source because Kingston is not interested in preserving discrete boundaries between myths and stories but in culling whatever is useful in "my American life" (Islas 14).

Kingston transforms various elements of *The Water Margin*, *Romance of the Three Kingdoms*, and *Journey to the West* in order to subvert common stereotypes and assumptions. To one listener, Wittman describes his play as a revision of *The Water Margin* (*TM* 261). Kingston focuses on *The Water Margin*'s 108 bandits to create an image of a cohesive, rebellious Chinese American community that challenges the damaging stereotype of the "model minority." The secret to a strong Chinese American community, Wittman insists, lies in this redefinition of Chinese Americans as outlaws. By putting on a show about the 108 bandits, the community becomes, in a tricksterlike move of resistance, at once a group of outcasts and a force to be reckoned with. During the performance the narrator boldly dares the sheriff to arrest the actors for disturbing the peace, describing with pride and defiance a history of Chinese Americans as victorious outlaws and tricksters:

> Jail us for performing without a permit, like our brave the-
> atrical ancestors, who were violators of zoning ordinances;
> they put on shows, they paraded, they raised chickens within
> city limits. They were flimflammers of tourists, wildcat min-
> ers . . . aliens unqualifiable to apply for citizenship, unrelated

> communalists and crowders into single-family dwellings,
> dwellers and gamblers in the backs of stores, restaurateurs
> and launderers who didn't pass health inspections . . .
> payers and takers of less than minimum wage . . . dodgers
> of the draft of several countries, un-Americans, red-hot
> communists, unbridled capitalists, look-alikes of japs and
> Viet Cong, unlicensed manufacturers and exploders of
> fireworks. Everybody with aliases. More than one hundred
> and eight outlaws. (*TM* 301–302)

This long catalogue (of which I have quoted only half) rewrites Chinese American history, presenting it not as a story of victimization and oppression but as a celebration of artful dodgers of the system, who preserved their spirit, their sense of fun, and their will to survive despite unjust labels and unjust laws. Kingston implicitly addresses her own critics when she overturns Grand Opening Ah Sing's fears that Wittman's play will be "bad advertising" for Chinese American culture: creating a sense of shared history, she makes "outlaw" a source of communal identity and pride.

Kingston's use of the war epic *The Romance of the Three Kingdoms* also allows her to revise aspects of her Chinese American heritage in important ways, in particular by suggesting that trickster strategies—storytelling, jokes, and performance—provide a more viable way of fighting social injustice and building community than does violence. Wittman learns through his production of *The Romance of the Three Kingdoms* that this war epic contains an antiwar message (*TM* 340).[25] *Tripmaster Monkey* is set during the United States's escalating involvement in Vietnam, and the novel is partly about Wittman's efforts to avoid the draft, even as he wages a private war on racism.[26] The dramatized war, then, provides a constructive rather than destructive outlet for real anger and real wars (*TM* 306). Kingston implicitly associates Wittman's staged war with both racial violence and Vietnam, connecting Wittman's staged fireworks to the Watts riot fires and connecting Vietnam draft dodging to the Chinese Americans hiding out after the L.A. Massacre, which killed nineteen (*TM* 306, 340). Through performance and storytelling, the play and the novel (the "fake war" recalling the "fake book" of the title) release anger, pain, and frustration caused by racism, as well as desperation and mistrust of the American political system engendered by the Vietnam War.[27]

The epic *Journey to the West* also undergoes a metamorphosis in *Tripmaster Monkey*. Kingston uses her version of this famous trickster legend to blast the common stereotype of Chinese Americans as temporary sojourners, or foreigners, in America. "All you saw was West," Wittman says of his play. "This is The Journey *in* the West" (*TM* 308). Whereas the west in the popular American imagination symbolizes the opportunity and adventure of the frontier, the west in the popular Chinese imagination is the western paradise to which Monkey and Tripitaka travel in a quest for enlightenment and fame (Chua 146). Kingston's collapse of the two into "Journey in the West" not only reiterates that there's "nobody here but us Americans" (*TM* 309) but also ironically comments on Chinese immigrants' search for a Gold Mountain in America.

Kingston's other major adaptation of *Journey to the West* concerns *Tripmaster Monkey*'s narrative voice. Both fiercely protective of Wittman and quite critical of him, the novel's mercurial narrator resembles Kuan Yin, the Goddess of Mercy who supervises Monkey's journey.[28] Kingston's choice of a Chinese American goddess narrator radically critiques the Anglo-American narrative tradition of a white male god and reminds us that neither point of view is neutral. Kuan Yin as narrator also represents a substantial revision of the original *Journey to the West*, in which Kuan Yin appears sporadically. By giving Kuan Yin voice and authorial control, Kingston creates a dialogic tension within the narrative, often explicitly challenging Wittman's sexism. For example, after Wittman tells the story of his stage-performance birth to his pretty Chinese American date Nanci Lee, Nanci begins to tell her own story of performing magic tricks as a child. Wittman's response, "What's this? She doing geisha shtick for me?" reveals his own entrapment in sexist, racist stereotyping (*TM* 17). The novel's narrator sharply prods, "You're not the only one, Wittman, who fooled with magic . . . and also not the only one to talk. She had to talk too, make this a conversation" (*TM* 17).

Since *Tripmaster Monkey* is a Journey *in* the West, its search for new, community-building stories involves a reworking not only of classic Chinese novels but also of American popular culture. Movies pose a huge threat to Chinese American cultural identity because they are such pervasive purveyors of damaging stereotypes ("All we do in the movies is die" [*TM* 323]), yet at the same time they carry enormous potential for culture building. Wittman expends much dramatic energy in critiquing the damaging stereotypes of Chinese Americans in popular culture and in finding ways to celebrate and emphasize Chinese American participation in American culture. He advocates trickster strategies for actors in stereotyped roles: "Pass messages. 'Eat shit, James Bond'" (*TM* 325). He revises American film history to find evidence of Chinese American participation, noting the "Chinese eyes" of cowboy heroes in western films (*TM* 314). Yet recognizing Chinese traits in Caucasian stars is not enough; it doesn't fulfill Wittman's search for a Chinese American role model in popular culture, someone who will teach him "how to hold my face" (*TM* 324). Finally Wittman realizes that he must create new roles for all those left out of the "Hogan Tyrone Loman Big Daddy family" and revise the Eugene O'Neill and Arthur Miller theatrical canon to reflect his own experience of American culture (*TM* 25).

◎

Movies in *Tripmaster Monkey* provide models not only for cultural critique but also for the narrative process. *The Saragossa Manuscript*, as told in *Tripmaster Monkey*, becomes a model for a contemporary form of talk-story and for the transformative possibilities of art. Charley's retelling of the film is an intricate metaphor for and guide to *Tripmaster Monkey* and to life. The "story inside a story inside a story inside a story" contains "tricksters" who "change costumes and rearrange their poses" between scenes, and the movie itself contains layers of "hoodwink" that the viewer must break through (*TM* 102). Charlie realizes in successive viewings of the film that "between scenes and cuts and juxtapositions are strict cause-and-effect links. Nothing is missing. The main link chain, though, is spoken" (*TM* 102).

We might say the same thing about *Tripmaster Monkey*. Despite its apparently loose, anecdotal construction, each juxtaposition intricately signifies on its context, and orally transmitted talk-stories link the episodes together. The movie inspires a vision of human interaction as a web of interconnected stories, suggesting to Charley that "we are connected to one another in time and by blood. Each of us is so related, we're practically the same person living infinite versions of the great human adventure." Charley explains that "as I walked home . . . I understood that inside each door and window someone was leading an entire amazing life. . . . I can follow anybody into a strange other world. He or she will lead the way to another part of the story we're all inside of" (*TM* 103). The narrator of *Tripmaster Monkey* reiterates this idea: "Here we are, miraculously on Earth at the same moment, walking in and out of one another's lifestories, no problems of double exposure, no difficulties crossing the frame. Life is ultimately fun and doesn't repeat and doesn't end" (*TM* 103). This vision validates the novel's structure, which is full of snapshots of other lives, other perspectives. The notion that each person is the protagonist in his or her own life describes Kingston's purpose in constructing a multivocal, tricksterlike narrative that subverts the comfortable notion of a central character or a unified identity. Although "we're all inside of" the same story, each person can only tell a part of it, in much the same way that the girl in *The Woman Warrior* can only infer the whole dragon from a few visible parts. The movie has indeed helped "cure" Wittman, who comes away from Charley's performance with the feeling that "Yes, life is tricky and thick" (*TM* 103). So, too, is *Tripmaster Monkey.*

Charley's emphasis on what happened to him after he left the cinema—"I am a changed person. It's been two years, and I continue changing" (*TM* 100)—underlines a central emphasis in *Tripmaster Monkey* on the social and political aspects of creative production: the ability of art to effect change. As the movie cures Wittman, reviving in him a sense of possibility and connection, so the novel works to effect the same change in the reader. As Wittman is the trickster protagonist of *Tripmaster Monkey*, working to create a fictional community through his retelling of stories, so Kingston is *Tripmaster Monkey*'s trickster author, stepping in and out of various perspectives, catching her reader in successive layers of hoodwink, and inviting the reader to join the "community" of her novel.

Kingston draws a parallel between the changing aims of Wittman's and her own artistic careers: they both begin as poets and move toward more social art forms (M. Chin 61). Whereas the flesh-and-blood immediacy of theater makes playwriting clearly a social art, the novel has its own power to engage its audience. Kingston prizes the tricksterlike ability of the written word to cross boundaries that real social interactions cannot. "Words can get through all kinds of barriers," Kingston comments; "they can get through skin color and culture" (Fishkin 787). Through the gender- and color-blind medium of print, Kingston reaches readers whose entrapment in stereotyped thinking might otherwise prevent her from reaching.[29]

TRIPMASTER KINGSTON: THE AUTHOR AS TRICKSTER

Kingston's choice of a male trickster as a protagonist enables her to become a trickster as well. The complex interweaving of Wittman's male and Kuan Yin's female narrative voices allows the author an androgynous point of view. Kingston values the liberating potential of androgyny, citing William Carlos Williams's motherly Abraham Lincoln in *In the American Grain* and Virginia Woolf's androgynous *Orlando* as inspirations in her own writing (Fishkin 784). Rather than having been "taken over by an alien voice" in *Tripmaster Monkey*, as one critic suggests (Ling 153), Kingston writes as an androgynous trickster, giving voice to that "wild inventive sixties language" that is not only Wittman's but also her own (Fishkin 789).[30]

Kingston uses other characters to undercut Wittman's perspective, a technique that emphasizes the impossibility of any stable viewpoint. Wittman's wife, Taña, is tricksterlike, "a wanderfooting woman" as free as he is, one who refuses to cook or clean for him, thereby challenging his sexist expectations about her wifely duties (*TM* 161). In the middle of Wittman's tirade against the evils of racism, Nanci whispers to Auntie Marleese, "Poor Wittman . . . He's so oversensitive" (*TM* 320). Kingston complicates the issue of racism by making Wittman occasionally racist himself, and by reminding Wittman and his compatriots of their own double standards: "'You guys feel so sorry for youself,' said Auntie Dolly. 'But you tell tit twat cunt chick hom sup low jokes' (*TM* 317). As in *The Woman Warrior*, there are no easy ways to separate good from evil, right from wrong, racists from nonracists.

Finally, Kingston as a trickster author emphasizes the role of art in creating community. She accentuates the reader's role as audience in order to heighten a sense of participation in the text. A description of Wittman writing his play becomes an accurate description of the novel's development: "He spent the rest of the night looking for the plot of our ever-branching lives. A job can't be the plot of life, and not a soapy love-marriage-divorce—and hell no, not Viet Nam. To entertain and educate the solitaries that make up a community, the play will be a combination revuelecture. You're invited" (*TM* 288). The narrator's direct invitation to the reader underscores our relationship to the fictional theatergoers. Kingston invites us to read her novel as if we were attending a play. Her frequent direct addresses to the reader emphasize the novel's affinity to oral performance and echo a similar device in *Journey to the West* and other classic Chinese novels. As Wittman learns with successive performances of his play, storytelling creates community: "Wittman was learning that one big bang-up show has to be followed up with a second show, a third show, shows until something takes hold. He was defining a community, which will meet every night for a season. Community is not built once-and-for-all; people have to imagine, practice and recreate it" (*TM* 306). The idea that we must "imagine, practice and recreate" community reiterates the dynamic status of community and the need for continually revising traditional myths in a contemporary context.[31]

However, far from idealizing community as an easy solution, Kingston emphasizes the difficulties involved in creating and maintaining a cohesive community that preserves the individuality of its members. The form of the play itself suggests a vision of community in which identity and unity might be reconciled. Rather than attempting to present a monolithic front, the play (like the novel's structure) is a "revue" that encompasses a diversity of perspectives. The gathering of Wittman's friends, relatives, and acquaintances for the production, to which each contributes not just a role but his or her own creative voice, closely approximates Kingston's ideal of the multivocal novel. Highlighting the current conflicts within the Asian American literary community, Wittman's friend Lance interprets Wittman's invitation to his play as a challenge and brings his own gang and his own script to the rehearsal. The play can only be a success, Kingston suggests, with "lots of holes for ad lib and actors' gifts" that ensure a multivoiced presentation in which everyone has his or her say (*TM* 279).

Kingston challenges us to consider our own role in this story-telling performance by highlighting the fictional audience and the reviewers of Wittman's play. Wittman begins his "One-Man Show" on the third night by castigating his reviewers. The tirade restates—in more colorful language—Kingston's own frustrations with reviewers of *The Woman Warrior*, published in "Cultural Mis-Readings by American Reviewers." Having explained in "Cultural Mis-Readings" that "to say we are inscrutable, mysterious, exotic denies us our common humanness" (57), Kingston has Wittman reiterate more angrily in *Tripmaster Monkey*, "I am so fucking offended. . . . Do I have to explain why 'exotic' pisses me off, and 'not exotic' pisses me off? They've got us in a bag, which we aren't punching our way out of " (*TM* 308). The inclusion of this critique in her novel is a literary trick; despite Kingston's sense of frustration that such explanations are necessary, her inscribed critique of stereotyped reviewing educates her critics about how to respond to her novel, forestalling future mis-readings of her work.

By having Wittman educate her critics, Kingston plays a literary trick on her most vocal and vitriolic critic within the Chinese American literary community, Frank Chin. Many critics have noted, and Kingston admits, that Wittman's character is partly based on Chin (Ling 149). Using Wittman as a personal parody of Chin allows Kingston to appropriate his voice to attack and dispel western stereotypes, the very things Chin accuses Kingston of propagating in her work. The author as trickster surpasses the boundaries of fiction to play tricks on her contemporaries. Kingston's parody of Chin responds, though with considerably less bitterness than the original, to Chin's parody of Kingston and *The Woman Warrior*, "The Most Popular Book in

China," printed as the afterword to his short story collection, *The Chinaman Pacific and Frisco Railroad Company. Tripmaster Monkey*'s subtitle, *His Fake Book*, also ironically responds to Chin's classification of Kingston's work as "fake" Chinese American ("Come All Ye" 1–10).

Kingston focuses attention on readers' reactions to her novel by heightening our awareness of audience response to Wittman's play. Wittman aims to produce "an enormous loud play that will awake our audience, bring it back," recalling Thoreau's effort to "wake my neighbors up" (*TM* 277).[32] An audience, of course, is not always so easily roused. The narrator explains during Wittman's monologue that "he was losing some audience. . . . They love fight scenes; they love firecrackers. But during a soliloquy when a human being is thinking out how to live, everybody walks about, goes to the can, eats, visits. O audience" (*TM* 333). By focusing on audience participation in a play that is so like her own novel, Kingston makes the reader conscious of his or her own reactions. In a tricksterlike effort to poke holes through the invisible screen separating fiction from life, Kingston continually highlights the motivations of willful misreaders. For example, Wittman's critique of women who cosmetically or surgically alter their eyelids produces a range of reactions among his audience and thereby raises questions about the extent to which even a direct assault can reach its intended audience. After Wittman mocks fake eyelashes and taped lids, plain

> Judy . . . was agreeing with him, nodding her natural head.
> And Taña, who did not have an eye problem, also understood.
> She would let that tactless husband of hers have it later in private. The ladies with the mink eyelashes ought to speak up for themselves. But through the make-up they did not feel assaults

on their looks. . . . Wittman was just part of the show, which
did not upset them; he's talking about other girls. (*TM* 312)

The narrative voice here steps tricksterlike in and out of different perspectives. Such an extended examination of audience reaction, particularly of those who remain untouched, refracts the
reader's focus back onto his or her own reading process in order
to startle the detached reader into self-recognition.

Kingston celebrates blending of fiction and reality when
Wittman's play spills into the streets: "On cue—the S.F.F.D. was
bringing the redness and the wailing. . . . The audience ran out
into the street. More audience came. And the actors were out
from backstage and the green room, breaking rules of reality-
and-illusion. Their armor and swords were mirrored in fenders,
bumpers, and the long sides of the fire trucks. The clean clear red
metal glorified all that was shining" (*TM* 303). This fiasco turns
into a celebration and a victory, as Wittman artfully orchestrates
the chaos as a part of the act. The fire department's arrival enhances the drama and creates more audience and therefore a
larger potential community.

Significantly, Wittman stages the opening night of his play on
Halloween. Ralph Ellison has said that "America is a land of
masking jokers," and on Halloween, Kingston reminds us, "more
maskers were at large than ever" (*TM* 289).[33] Halloween, a night
of disguises and candy, is the nearest national holiday Americans
have to carnival, the trickster's realm. Wittman schedules his performance for the night when his own trickster power of masking
is at its height. Wittman calls Halloween "Hawk Guai Night . . .
Scare the Ghosts Night" (*TM* 262). Any reader familiar with *The
Woman Warrior* is sensitized to the Chinese American meaning of

ghosts as outsiders, particularly whites. His play, designed to "spook out racism" and startle his audience with comic, outrageous, unflattering images of themselves, is a move to "scare" the racist ghosts (*TM* 332).

"Somehow," Kingston says, "we are going to solve the world's problems with fun and theater. And with laughter" (M. Chin 61). Wittman's audience interprets his divorce announcement as a marriage announcement, producing a comic happy ending with an interracial marriage and an image of community celebration. This interracial marriage is a double-edged sword, suggesting both interracial harmony and a fundamental rift between Chinese American men and women. "She's not Chinese, I'll admit, but those girls are all out with white guys," Wittman says (*TM* 336). The lack of communication between Chinese American men and women, Kingston feels, is a problem that remains to be solved.[34] Kingston clearly maintains hope in the power of a community to strengthen its members. "Given heart by a loving community," Wittman confides his joys, pain, and anger, and in doing so he renews and transforms his American culture with new, powerful myths (*TM* 331).

True to its Monkey spirit, *Tripmaster Monkey* is an inventive, renewing, participatory text. Rather than pretend to resolve all conflict, Kingston's work suggests an expansive view of reality that allows for a diversity of perspectives. Kingston's writing shows the redemptive power of the trickster, not only aesthetically but also culturally and personally. The trickster transforms narrative structure, creates new cultural myths, and extends the boundaries of the self. Through layers of hoodwink, verbal fireworks, and a dynamic, inclusive definition of community, Kingston's works remind us that "Yes, life is tricky and thick."

CHAPTER THREE

Comic Liberators and Word-Healers

The Interwoven Trickster Narratives of
Louise Erdrich

The trickster's constant chatterings and antics remind us that
life is endlessly narrative, prolific and openended.
                    William Hynes, Mythical Trickster Figures

From the first publication of *Love Medicine* in 1984, tricksters
have played a central and pervasive role in Louise Erdrich's fiction.[1] A family of tricksters wanders through *Love Medicine*,
Tracks, and *The Bingo Palace*. The very existence of such a trickster "family" as Erdrich's rewrites a major tenet of a trickster tradition in which the trickster always travels alone. Erdrich's novels transgress trickster traditions in other ways as well, revising
traditional myths, and in the cases of Fleur and Lulu, combining
parts of several myths and pushing the limits of our conception

of the trickster. Erdrich's tricksters can't be contained, whether in a body, in a prison, in a single story or novel, or—as the expanded 1993 edition of *Love Medicine* suggests—even in a particular version of a novel.

Several of Erdrich's characters bear important resemblances to Chippewa trickster Nanabozho, and her work offers a trickster-inspired view of identity, community, history, and narrative. As the community evolves, so do the novels' narrative forms. Indeed, the evolving narrative forms of *Love Medicine, Tracks,* and *The Bingo Palace* express the history of a Chippewa community in trickster terms that, far from reinforcing stereotypes of a vanishing tribe, emphasize variety, vibrancy, and continuance. Tricksters' ability to escape virtually any situation and survive any adventure makes them particularly appealing to an artist like Erdrich, who feels that Native American writers, "in the light of enormous loss, must tell the stories of contemporary survivors, while protecting and celebrating the cores of cultures left in the wake of the catastrophe ("Where" 23). Through trickster characters and a trickster aesthetic, Erdrich attests to the personal and cultural survival of the Chippewa people.

In Erdrich's works, tricksters are central to the formulation of identity, the creation of community, and the preservation of culture. Through their courageous, outrageous stories, their transgressions not only of law and convention but also of flesh and blood, Erdrich's tricksters are, to borrow Gerald Vizenor's words, "enchanter[s], comic liberator[s], and word healer[s]" (*Trickster of Liberty* x). Erdrich's works convey a tricksterlike delight in the margin as a place of connection and transformation. Her novels focus our attention on these interconnections, not only between characters but also among the various stories and across the novels. The new and expanded version of *Love Medicine* heightens and reinforces the interconnections among the novels, while questioning the stability of the novel as a form. In keeping with Erdrich's aesthetic of interconnection, my discussion focuses first on the trickster's relationship to identity and then on the trickster-inspired narrative structures that link family, the community, and the novels.

TRICKSTER IDENTITY: *LOVE MEDICINE* AND *TRACKS*

That tricksters inspire Erdrich's formulation of identity may appear at first a risky claim. After all, the trickster embodies paradox; his or her ever-shifting form seems to negate the possibility of any "stable" identity. Yet paradox is a part of Native American (and postmodern) conceptions of identity, and the shiftiness defines the trickster's identity. If aptly directed, Erdrich suggests, a trickster-inspired view of identity can be liberating and empowering. Traditionally, the Chippewa trickster Nanabozho is "the master of life—the source and impersonation of the lives of all sentient things, human, faunal, and floral. . . . He was regarded as the master of ruses but also possessed great wisdom in the prolonging of life" (Densmore 97). As the "master of ruses," Nanabozho wields as his chief weapon the power of transformation. Nanabozho could "assume at will . . . a new form, shape, and existence"; he "could be a man, and change to a pebble in the next instant. He could be a puff of wind, a cloud fragment, a flower, a toad" (Johnston 19–20). Using his transformational powers to escape from difficult situations and attack his enemies, Nanabozho's transformational ability implies control over his physical boundaries. It is the trickster's questioning of physical boundaries that is central to Erdrich's vision of identity based on connections to myth and community.

As I argue elsewhere in detail, Erdrich views identity as "transpersonal": a strong sense of self must be based not on isolation but on personal connections to community and to myth (see Smith). In *Love Medicine*, Erdrich translates the concept of a fluid, transpersonal identity in concretely physical terms: bodies become boundaries, outer layers that limit and define individuals. Characters flow out of their bodies and open themselves up to engulf the world. Even death does not contain them. Those characters gifted with Nanabozho's ability to control, or dissolve, their own physical boundaries have the strongest identities.

On the night of her homecoming at the beginning of *Love Medicine*, Albertine Johnson experiences a mystical merging with the northern lights as she lies in a field next to her cousin Lipsha. Her description shows how a physical connection to myth, community, and the landscape provides strength.

> Northern lights. Something in the cold, wet atmosphere brought them out. I grabbed Lipsha's arm. We floated into the field and sank down. . . . Everything seemed to be one piece. The air, our faces, all cool, moist, and dark, and the ghostly sky. . . . At times the whole sky was ringed in shooting points . . . pulsing, fading, rhythmical as breathing . . . as if the sky were a pattern of nerves and our thoughts and memories traveled across it . . . one gigantic memory for us all. (*LM* 37)[2]

Albertine's vision of a vast, universal brain, of which her own face forms a part, expresses what William Bevis calls "transpersonal time and space" (585). Everything connects and interrelates in living, breathing patterns and rhythms that Albertine inhabits both physically and mentally.

Albertine's vision strikingly parallels one of Nanabozho, as described by the Chippewa writer Edward Benton-Banai:

> As he rested in camp that night, Waynaboozhoo looked up into the sky and was overwhelmed at the beauty of the ah-nung-ug (stars).[3] They seemed to stretch away forever into the Ish-pi-ming (Universe). He became lost in the vast expanse of the stars. . . . Waynaboozhoo sensed a pulse, a rhythm in the Universe of stars. He felt his own o-day (heart) beating within himself. The beat of his heart and the beat of the Universe were the same. Waynaboozhoo gazed into the stars with joy. He drifted off to sleep listening to his heart and comforted by the feeling of oneness with the rhythm of the Universe. (56–57)

Like Albertine, Nanabozho in this story is lonely and confused. For both, the merging experience counteracts a sense of alienation and disconnectedness. Albertine's vision is powerful because it reestablishes her sense of connection to her home landscape, to her family (she holds Lipsha's arm and they float together), and, importantly, to Chippewa myth. Seeing the northern lights, Albertine imagines the sky as "a dance hall. And all the world's wandering souls were dancing there. I thought of June. She would be dancing if there were a dancehall in space" (*LM* 37). In Chippewa myth the joyful dancing of the dead in the afterworld creates the northern lights.[4] Albertine's vision places June within a community, in a "dancehall in space," and reestablishes her own links to her culture. By reinforcing her transpersonal and mythic connections to her family, her community, and the natural universe, Albertine's physical merging into the cool, dark night intensifies her own sense of identity.

Albertine's single tricksterlike visionary experience is typical of Erdrich's technique; rather than assign a trickster identity to one particular character who has multiple trickster attributes, she emphasizes the trickster's multifaceted identity with an array of trickster characters. Nanabozho most clearly appears in *Love Medicine* in the magically flexible form of his namesake, Gerry Nanapush. As the novel's most conspicuous embodiment of the trickster, Gerry addresses Erdrich's central concerns by challenging the notion of fixed boundaries, both physically with his transformative powers and politically with his continual escapes from imprisonment by whites. Chippewa writer and critic Gerald Vizenor describes Nanabozho as a "comic healer and liberator" ("Trickster Discourse" 188). Gerry Nanapush fits both of these descriptions insofar as he represents Erdrich's concern with liberating and healing Chippewa culture from damaging white stereotypes. A thoroughly modern trickster, the two-hundred-and-fifty-pound Gerry squirms through prison walls and vanishes in thin air in *Love Medicine*, garnering his trickster reputation as a "famous politicking hero, dangerous armed criminal, judo expert, escape artist, charismatic member of the American Indian Movement, and smoker of many pipes of kinnikinnick in the most radical groups" (*LM* 341). Because it allows him to escape both literal and figurative confinement, the trickster's transformative power takes on political importance in *Love Medicine*.

Originally imprisoned because of a bar fight with a cowboy over a racial slur, Gerry ends up in jail because, as Albertine Johnson dryly observes,

White people are good witnesses to have on your side, because they have names, addresses, social security numbers, and work phones. But they are terrible witnesses to have against you, almost as bad as having Indians witness for you. Not only did Gerry's friends lack all forms of identification except their band cards, not only did they disappear (out of no malice but simply because Gerry was tried during powwow time), but the few he did manage to get were not interested in looking judge or jury in the eyes. . . . Gerry's friends, you see, had no confidence in the United States judicial system. (*LM* 201)

By placing her Nanabozho figure in such a conflict, Erdrich suggests the trickster's power to counteract and heal the wounds of racial injustice. Andrew Wiget points out that the ability to change form is an essential survival strategy against such restrictive forces: "Trickster is in the business of . . . insuring that man remains 'unfinished' by fossilized institutions, open and adaptable instead to changing contemporary realities' (21). Gerry keeps escaping, true to his proud slogan that "no concrete shit-barn prison's built that can hold a Chippewa" (*LM* 341). His face on protest buttons and the six o'clock news, he galvanizes the Chippewa community with his miraculous getaways, sailing out of three-story windows and flying up airshafts, which liberate him and by extension all Chippewas from the white world's effort to contain and define them.

The "unfinished" nature of the trickster provides an escape from essentializing definitions; however strong the mythic dimensions of Gerry's character, Erdrich carefully emphasizes his humanity as well. As Greg Sarris suggests, pinning a trickster identity onto Gerry would be just as confining as all of the stereotypes from which he struggles to break free (130).[5] With a deft sleight of hand, Erdrich shatters any static image of Gerry as trickster by showing the toll Gerry's public trickster role has taken as he awaits the birth of his daughter: "All the quickness and delicacy of his movements had disappeared, and he was only a poor tired fat man in those hours, a husband worried about his wife, menaced, tired of getting caught" (*LM* 168). Although he escapes from prison again in *The Bingo Palace*, his appearance in that novel makes over-romanticizing him impossible; physically diminished by years in a maximum security prison, Gerry's much-changed image on the television screen shocks his friend Albertine. Whereas the old Gerry "had absorbed and cushioned insults with a lopsided jolt of humor, . . . had been a man whose eyes lighted, who shed sparks," his gaze in a prison life documentary strikes her as hungry and desperate (*BP* 24–25). Erdrich's characterization of Gerry forces readers to consider both the mythic and the psychological dimensions of identity.[6]

Given the fact that the trickster, as Vizenor explains, is a "teacher and healer in various personalities," Gerry's clownish, bumbling son, Lipsha, is clearly another of *Love Medicine*'s tricksters, deriving his healing "touch" from his mythical forebear ("People" 4). His uncle Lyman describes him as "a wild jack . . . clever and contriving as a fox," and, as a trickster in the youngest Chippewa generation, Lipsha represents the hope of cultural survival (*LM* 304). He goes on to become a central character in Erdrich's most recent novel *The Bingo Palace* (1994), in which he wavers (tricksterlike) between the luck and easy money of gambling and the fear that turning reservation lands into casino property will rob his community of its heritage and sense of identity.

In the title chapter of *Love Medicine*, Erdrich comically recasts the Nanabozho origin myth in the story of Lipsha's search for his parents.[7] In the myth, when Nanabozho learns from his grandmother Nookomis that his mother had been stolen by a "powerful wind spirit" at his birth, he sets out on a long journey to find her and finally meets the great gambler, with whom he battles over the destiny of his people. At the tale's end, Nanabozho beats the gambler through trickery and returns to his people triumphant. The parallels to *Love Medicine* are clear. Like Nanabozho, Lipsha Morrissey first learns about his parents through his grandmother, Lulu Lamartine. Lipsha's mother, June, has also disappeared in a powerful wind (swept up in a North Dakota snowstorm), and after a search he finally meets his own trickster father, Gerry, and the traitorous King Kashpaw. The three gamble for King's car, and the father and son tricksters emerge victorious. Lipsha's repetition of Nanabozho's journey underscores the importance Erdrich places on cultural survival and suggests the danger betrayers like King pose to it. As with the Nanabozho myth, this poker game represents a struggle over the tribe's destiny, and by escaping from the police and winning King's car, Gerry and Lipsha outwit, if only for the moment, the internal and external forces that threaten to destroy the community. Erdrich's splitting of the trickster into two characters, the wandering Gerry and the homebound Lipsha, emphasizes the trickster's dual character as both marginal and central to the culture and underscores the trickster's multiple identity.[8]

Although Gerry's mother, Lulu Lamartine, corresponds to Nanabozho's grandmother Nookomis, Lulu is also Erdrich's feminist revisioning of the trickster, sharing Nanabozho's physical flexibility, artful gambling, and sexual prowess. Like the trickster, Lulu can "beat the devil himself at cards." She brags, "I am a woman of detachable parts" (*LM* 115). Always the center of gossip for transgressing societal rules, Lulu even breaks the incest taboo, pursuing and catching her distant cousin Moses Pillager in a union that produces her trickster son, Gerry. Like Gerry, Lulu has a history of escape from government institutions; as a child she repeatedly ran away from her government boarding school (*LM* 68). When she escapes the schools for good, thanks to the clever letters of her trickster grandfather, old man Nanapush, she revels in the thought that "they could not cage me anymore" (*LM* 69).

Though she does not narrate her own story until *Love Medicine*, Lulu provides a vital link between *Love Medicine* and *Tracks* as the listener to whom old man Nanapush's narration in *Tracks* is addressed. Through his stories, Nanapush counteracts the Indian boarding schools' attempts at cultural erasure and recreates a family and a tribal history for Lulu.[9] Lulu's nine children speak for the ultimate success of Nanapush's message, for she almost single-handedly repopulates the reservation, knitting the tribe into one big family through their many fathers (Van Dyke 20). Erdrich emphasizes this familial interconnectedness in her description of "Lulu's boys": "Their gangling legs, encased alike in faded denim, shifted as if a ripple went through them collectively. . . . Clearly they were of one soul. Handsome, rangy, wildly various, they were bound in total loyalty, not by oath but by the simple, unquestioning belongingness of part of one organism" (*LM* 118). Fostered by their trickster mother, the boys present a picture of a potentially competitive and explosive system of interrelationships unified and strengthened by a sense of unquestioning belongingness.

A transformer, Lulu possesses the trickster's ability to dissolve her physical boundaries and merge with and absorb her environment: "I'd open my mouth wide, my ears wide, my heart, and I'd let everything inside" (*LM* 276). Lulu questions even the possibility of imposing boundaries, and as with Gerry, her trickster qualities lead her to deliver a political message: "All through my life I never did believe in human measurement," she explains, "numbers, time, inches, feet. All are just ploys for cutting nature down to size. I know the grand scheme of the world is beyond our brains to fathom, so I don't try, just let it in. . . . If we're going to measure land, let's measure right. Every foot and inch you're standing on . . . belongs to the Indians" (*LM* 282). Though her sexual escapades win her a trickster's lowly reputation, Lulu's political awareness makes her a guardian of the culture. She warns the tribal council of selling land to the government for a "tomahawk factory [that] mocked us all. . . . Indian against Indian, that's how the government's money offer made us act" (*LM* 284, 283). By the end of *Love Medicine*, Lulu emerges as an "old-time traditional," a cultural leader whose outrageous behavior in no way lessens her influence (*LM* 363).

Uninhibited by social constraints, free to dissolve boundaries and break taboos, the trickster's position on the edges of culture makes her or his perspective inherently revolutionary. As an "animate principle of disruption," the trickster questions rigid definitions and boundaries and challenges cultural assumptions (Wiget 86). By emphasizing her characters' trickster traits, Erdrich turns stereotypically negative images into sources of strength and survival. Using Gerry's trickster characteristics to turn the threatening image of an escaped federal criminal into a symbol of human vitality and possibility, Erdrich also, through the resonance of the Nanabozho legend, transforms Lipsha's maladroit escape from home into a confirmation of personal and cultural identity. Finally, she makes us see Lulu not as the "heartless, shameless man-chaser" and "jabwa witch" that she is reputed to be, but as a woman of vibrancy and vision (*LM* 277, 322).

The oldest and most vocal of Erdrich's tricksters is old man Nanapush in *Tracks*, to whom Erdrich devotes over half of that novel's chapters. Nanapush has all the markings of a trickster: a joker, a healer, and a "clever gambler" who "satisfied three wives," he lives in a "tightly tamped box overlooking the crossroad" (*T* 38, 41, 4)[10] Though of an earlier generation, Nanapush shares with Lulu and Gerry the circumstance of having escaped from confinement in a white world, and significantly, he associates this escape directly with being a trickster: "I had a Jesuit education in the halls of Saint John before I ran back to the woods and forgot all my prayers. My father said, 'Nanapush. That's what you'll be called. Because it's got to do with trickery and living in the bush'" (*T* 33). Erdrich's repetition of this pattern of indoctrination and escape indicates its importance as a trickster strategy for cultural survival.

Nanapush's tricksterlike skill as a mediator between worlds has led several critics to emphasize his adaptability.[11] Certainly, survival depends upon adapting, yet in Erdrich's view adaptability can also lead to assimilation and even to a collapse of identity. Although Nanapush's knowledge of English makes him an authority within the tribe and a tribal representative to the government, his attitude toward his own bilingualism is deeply ambivalent. The trickster's transformational ability can only provide a useful model for identity when that fluid identity is firmly grounded in a sense of culture and place. For example, Nanapush's knowledge of American laws and language enable him to "reach through the loophole" and bring Lulu home from the government school (*T* 225). Yet Nanapush regards his own knowledge of written English warily, because he knows that adaptation to modern, western ways can mean the loss of cultural identity. As he observes, "We were becoming . . . a tribe of file cabinets and triplicates, a tribe of single-space documents, directives, policy. A tribe of pressed trees. A tribe of chicken-scratch that can be scattered by a wind, diminished to ashes by one struck match" (*T* 225). Adaptation without connection to one's home and culture undermines identity and threatens the community, as we see in Lyman Lamartine. Lyman's description of his own fragile identity in *Love Medicine* ironically fulfills Nanapush's prediction in *Tracks*. "I could die now and leave no ripple. Why not! I considered, but then I came up with the fact that my death would leave a gap in the BIA records, my IRS account would be labeled incomplete until it closed. . . . In cabinets of files, anyway, I still maintained existence. The government knew me though the wind and the earth did not. I was alive, at least on paper" (300). Reborn "out of papers," Lyman skillfully works his way up in the Bureau of Indian Affairs and goes on to build the very tomahawk factory that his mother, Lulu, had named a threat to traditional culture (*LM* 303).

Vividly illustrating this danger of adapting too completely, one Chippewa trickster tale recounts:

One morning Winabojo got up early and went into the woods. He saw a great many men with clubs and asked what they were doing. They replied, "We are going to get the boy that your people wagered in the game; you had better join us

or you will be killed." Winabojo decided to do this in order
to save his family. When they attacked the village he was so
eager that he went right to his own lodge and began to kill
his family. He killed the old people and the two boys and was
about to kill the baby girl when someone stopped him. Then
he was like someone waking from a dream and felt very sorry
for what he had done. (Densmore 99)

Winabojo identifies so completely with his enemies that he kills
his own family without realizing it, a vivid warning against internalized oppression.[12] The destruction of Lyman's tomahawk factory brings about a similar result when Lyman notices Marie
Kashpaw's hands have been mutilated in a machine designed to
reproduce the work of "a hundred Chippewa grandmothers"
(*LM* 310). Internalized racism sharply, if comically, colors Lyman's characterization of himself as "the flesh-and-blood proof
of Nector Kashpaw's teepee-creeping" and his characterization
of the activists in his community as "back-to-the-buffalo types"
(*LM* 303).[13] If such self-contempt and loss of identity is to be
avoided, then the fluidity that allows the trickster to adapt to
swiftly changing circumstances must spring from strong connections to community and culture.[14]

One character so closely connected to the myths and old language of the traditional Chippewa that she remains at the margins of Erdrich's contemporary fictional world is Fleur Pillager,
whose heroic fights to save her land, unconventional dress and
behavior, and mythic connections make her a compelling female
trickster figure. In addition to her pivotal role in *Tracks*, Fleur appears as an itinerant healer and powerful medicine woman in *The
Beet Queen*, *Love Medicine*, and *The Bingo Palace*; she is the only

character to appear in all four novels. That Erdrich revised *Love Medicine* to include Fleur in her 1993 edition underscores Fleur's importance to the series, connecting the novels through her marginal but powerful presence. If Gerry and Nanapush are Erdrich's most traditional and widely recognized tricksters, Fleur represents Erdrich's most dramatic revision of the trickster. With Fleur, Erdrich not only retells traditional myths but, like Maxine Hong Kingston, reinvents and combines them. Fleur transgresses traditional myths, combining elements of the wolf (Nanabozho's brother), Misshepeshu the Water Monster, and the bear, making new combinations that are necessary for survival.[15]

As Gerry does with Lipsha in *Love Medicine*, Fleur shares the trickster's role in *Tracks* with the verbose and socially central Nanapush, and like Gerry, Fleur never narrates. As Bonnie Tu-Smith notes, whereas Nanapush's trickster-outsider role is "sanctioned within the community" so that he "represents the communal voice" in the novel, Fleur escapes even the Chippewa community's attempts to define her, dressing like a man and living alone in spirit-inhabited woods (TuSmith, *All My Relatives* 131). Just as Gerry gains fame for his outlaw status, Fleur in an earlier time achieves an equally mythic reputation on the reservation and in nearby towns. "Power travels in the bloodlines," Pauline says, and although Fleur is not a blood relative of Nanapush, as his spiritual daughter she inherits his trickster traits along with the mystical powers of her own Pillager line (*T* 31). Unconventional as she is, Fleur displays traditional trickster behavior. She is sensual and skilled at cards and, like Nanapush, Lulu, and Gerry, Fleur encounters and escapes from a white world that attempts to define her too rigidly; she flees the small town of Argus after being raped by the three white men whom she beats at poker once too often. Like Lipsha's card game with King at the end of *Love Medicine*, Fleur's poker game with the men at the butcher shop represents a battle over the future of the tribe. By winning enough money to make tax payments on her land, she saves herself and her family from starvation.

However, Fleur's tricksterlike pride and independence alone are not enough to work miracles. She must journey, Nanabozho-like, to the afterworld to gamble for her second child's life, and ultimately she fails to save her family's ancestral lands. As with Gerry, Erdrich uses Fleur's trickster traits to show the mythic possibilities of real human beings and to emphasize the importance of community to survival. Nanapush gives us a reason for Fleur's failure that illuminates Erdrich's regard for community: "Power dies." Nanapush warns, "As soon as you rely on the possession it is gone. Forget that it ever existed, and it returns. I never made the mistake of thinking that I owned my own strength, that was my secret. And so I was never alone in my failures" (*T* 177). Human mythic strength, Nanapush suggests, demands community.

LONELY TRICKSTERS: *THE BEET QUEEN*

As if to reinforce the importance of community to a viable trickster identity, Erdrich introduces an alternative version of the trickster "family" in *The Beet Queen*. Karl and Mary Adare share many trickster traits, and even their estranged baby brother, Jude Miller, has "clever hands" (*BQ* 315). Yet in sharp contrast to the three novels set on the Chippewa reservation, this novel, set in the nearby town of Argus and containing mostly white characters, emphasizes the fragility of a trickster identity when not grounded in community and tradition.

The Beet Queen is only loosely connected to the tetralogy's other three novels.[16] Albertine's introduction of Dot Adare in *Love Medicine* foregrounds Erdrich's concern with community and cultural heritage: "On my left sat Gerry Nanapush of the Chippewa Tribe. On my right sat Dot Adare of the has-been, of the never-was, of the what's-in-front-of-me people" (*LM* 155). Dot is *The Beet Queen*'s title character, and the has-been never-was people to whom she belongs become the novel's central concern. If *The Beet Queen* pays tribute to Erdrich's German-American heritage and to her family's butcher shop, it also allows Erdrich to undercut the notion of any one family or community as "central" to her fictional world. Clearly, her focus on the Chippewa community in three novels speaks for the importance of Chippewa history and culture to her own art, but her departure from this locale in *The Beet Queen* deliberately decenters the tetralogy and allows her to explore other aspects of trickster identity. In *The Beet Queen*, Erdrich investigates what holds together identity, family, and community by repeatedly examining their collapse.

The Beet Queen opens with the explosion of a family, each fragment hurtling in a different direction. A single mother driven to desperation by debt and responsibility, Adelaide Adare flies off in a carnival plane in the novel's opening scene, abandoning her three children at an "Orphans' Picnic" (*BQ* 10). As the sun sets and the children realize their mother is not coming back, young Karl and Mary finally agree to let a stranger take their hungry baby brother home. They soon separate; Mary ends up in Argus searching for relatives, while Karl drifts aimlessly on railway boxcars.

Forced at a carnival (the trickster's realm) to face the chaos of having no ties, Karl and Mary struggle to define themselves with trickster strategies. Yet without a mythic structure such as the Nanabozho tradition on which to draw, their search is alienating and terrifying. Even among her relatives, Mary always feels an outsider, eventually finding solace in her fortune-telling tarot cards, Ouija boards, and yarrow sticks. Mary and Karl both embody the trickster's androgyny; at fourteen the bisexual Karl is mistaken for a girl, and Celestine James notes that "if you didn't know [Mary] was a woman you would never know it" (*BQ* 214). Mary's childhood is marked by one miraculous accident, when her headfirst dive down a playground slide into a sheet of ice produces a "miracle," the likeness of Christ.[17] Mary significantly sees not Christ's but Karl's face in the ice, which suggests his role as a double Christ-Satan figure in the novel, a suggestion that is later reinforced by Jude's recognizing Karl as "the devil" (*BQ* 82). Karl maintains a tricksterlike position in the church, practicing a double life in the seminary: "between the lines of sacred texts, I rendezvoused with thin hard hoboes who had slept in the bushes" (*BQ* 55).

Karl stands out as *The Beet Queen*'s most clearly developed trickster, turning his total loss of family into a fragile trickster identity. Karl becomes the trickster-as-con-man in his series of traveling salesman jobs; he meets lover Wallace Pfef while selling air seeders at a crop and livestock convention and later moves in with Celestine after trying to sell her a set of cheap knives. His rootlessness comes from having been torn away from his roots as a child, and he uses the trickster's wanderer identity to avoid human contact. Faced with the possibility of a genuine connection with Wallace, he is haunted by a fear of again losing physical (and psychological) reference to the world: "I suddenly had the feeling that had always frightened me, the blackness, the ground I'd stood on giving way, the falling no place" (*BQ* 106). His trickster identity—traveling light, no ties, no responsibility, no pain—relies on a lack of connections that leads eventually to his breakdown: "I made less and less sense too, until I made none at all. I was part of the senseless landscape. A pulse, a strip, of light. I give nothing, take nothing, mean nothing, hold nothing" (*BQ* 318).[18] Karl's view of a "senseless landscape" contrasts sharply with the intense, historically grounded relationship to land evident in all of Erdrich's Chippewa novels. For the dispossessed, land becomes increasingly precious, but Karl remains oblivious to the landscape's history. In this novel, Erdrich shows the meaninglessness to which a lack of connection to culture and community leads. Despite Karl's collapse, Erdrich ends *The Beet Queen* on a note of hope; Karl returns to Argus looking for Dot and finds Wallace. He is still a trickster, "disreputable, unshaven, unwashed, . . . hungry," and Dot notices his car is "backed into its parking place, ready for a smooth exit"; yet for the moment, he has reestablished the links (*BQ* 321, 338).

From the initial collapse of a family, the novel continually balances on the edge of connection and isolation, convergence and dispersion.[19] The characters are all "marginal" in a small midwestern town: Karl is bisexual, Wallace is homosexual, Celestine is part Native American, Sita is mentally ill, Mary is just unusual, and Dot is a social misfit. Together, they form "a complicated house" like that of the spider who makes its web in baby Dot's hair (*BQ* 204). Their links are tenuous, even hostile, clustered as they are around their possessive love for Dot. "More than anything we had in common, Dot's spite drove Celestine, Mary, and me together," Wallace Pfef notes (*BQ* 301). In one of the novel's final scenes, Dot reenacts her grandmother Adelaide's flight at the fair as she boards the skywriter's plane. As the crowds leave the grandstand, Karl, Celestine, Mary, and Wallace remain: "They made a little group, flung out of nowhere, but together. They did not lower their eyes, but kept watching as above them Dot's name slowly spread, broke apart in air currents, and was sucked into the stratosphere, letter by letter" (*BQ* 328). This image captures both convergence (the little group flung together) and dispersion (Dot's name disappearing in air) and thus reflects the frailty and preciousness of human relationships. Unlike her grandmother, however, Dot returns and heads home with her mother—a final, powerful note of connection in a novel that repeatedly stresses loneliness and disconnection.

EVOLVING COMMUNITY, EVOLVING NOVELS: THE TRICKSTER'S COMMUNAL VOICES

If the trickster exerts a slippery, indefinable, indefatigable presence in Erdrich's Chippewa novels, trickster energy also inspires the novels' forms. Alan Velie writes that "the only reservation that one might have in calling *Love Medicine* a trickster novel is that Gerry Nanapush is not really the central character" (122–123). Yet, paradoxically, it is Gerry's marginality that makes *Love Medicine* a trickster novel. Despite, or because of, their multivocality, Erdrich's novels embody a trickster aesthetic. The decentered narrative structure of her novels challenges an ethnocentric worldview with its multiple perspectives, which emphasize community, recreate the novel as a social storytelling process, and draw in the reader as one of the community of listeners. The issues of personal and cultural survival that Erdrich foregrounds with her emphasis on the trickster are inextricably connected to the process of communal storytelling that makes up the novels.

Love Medicine's narrative structure fulfills the trickster's function to unsettle or critique our worldview, by forcing us to "pause 'between worlds' to discover the arbitrary structural principles of both" (Rainwater 407). Yet Erdrich's approach to multiple narrative does more than create a postmodern, jarring effect. Unlike many postmodern novels, Erdrich's narrative forms create a vivid sense of community.[20] In *Love Medicine*, *Tracks*, and *The Bingo Palace*, Erdrich connects the literary techniques of multiple narrative to Native American oral traditions and, specifically, to oral storytelling techniques. Robert Silberman notes that Erdrich's work seems "at times to aspire to the status of 'pure' storytelling" in which, he explains, the literary text appears to be a direct transcription of a speaker addressing a particular listener (112).[21] With its shifts between ten different perspectives, including six first-person narrators, *Love Medicine* expresses community. The various voices and perspectives that make up its chapters emphasize both friction and harmony and place each individual's narrative in the context of a collective, communal narrative.

The creation of community through multiple narrative is an inherently tricksterlike process. The trickster's multivalence and elusiveness suggest that although no one point of view is all-encompassing, all points of view, including those of the author, the narrators, the characters, and the reader or listener, together create the meaning of the story, and this emphasizes the importance of dialogue and community to the storytelling process. Gerald Vizenor sees the trickster's function in Native American oral tales as "a consonance of narrative voices in discourse," an apt description for *Love Medicine*'s decentered, multivocal narrative structure ("Trickster Discourse" 193). The trickster, who dwells in and embodies the liminal, represents a site of intersection, dialogue, and connection even while eluding fixed definitions. The sometimes conflicting, sometimes coinciding narratives that form the chapters of *Love Medicine* create an implicit dialogue among the characters and a connection or an exchange within the narrative structure itself.

The reader of a trickster text like *Love Medicine* plays an integral part in the creation of meaning by sorting out and interpreting the various points of view, mapping the saga's various interconnected family trees, filling in gaps, and making the connections that none of the individual narrators make for us. Thus we can see the form of the book itself as healing, because in it the voices are united and, through the reading process, they appear to talk to each other.[22] As Kathleen Sands observes, "The best works of American Indian fiction are never passive; they demand that we enter not only into the fictional world but participate actively in the process of storytelling" (24). This is especially true of trickster texts like Erdrich's. The trickster, Gerald Vizenor posits, "liberates the mind" as the active reader "implies the author, imagines narrative voices, inspires characters, and salutes tribal tricksters in a comic discourse" (*Trickster of Liberty* x). Erdrich duplicates an oral storytelling situation through her multivocal narrative form: the reader, as a "listener," creates the occasion for each narrator's performance and becomes not only a part of an imagined community of listeners but an active participant in the creation of that community. Sands describes the experience of reading *Love Medicine* in tricksterlike terms:

As marginal and edged, episodic and juxtaposed as this narrative is, it is not the characters or events of the novel that are dislocated and peripheral. Each is central to an element of the narrative. It is the reader who is placed at a distance, who is the observer on the fringes of the story, forced to shift position, turn, ponder, and finally integrate the story into a coherent whole by recognizing the indestructible connections between the characters and events of the narrative(s). Hence the novel places the reader in a paradoxically dual stance, simultaneously on the fringe of the story yet at the very center of the process. (12)

Like the trickster, the reader is constantly shifting positions, on the fringe and yet central to the creation of meaning.

A multiple narrative may be especially effective in works aimed at multiple audiences, including Chippewa, pan-tribal, and non-Native readers. As James Ruppert notes, through multiple narratives, contemporary Native American authors can "speak to all audiences at the same time and at different levels," forcing all readers to "acknowledge the multiplicity of realities around them" and to develop a "mythic imagination" (224). It is through an accretion of various versions of the story that characters like Gerry and Fleur emerge as magical, mythical, and yet psychologically realistic characters. That there exist not just numerous versions of reality but a multiplicity of realities becomes, as we shall see, even more important to the community-based narrative structure of *Tracks*.

Though *Love Medicine* and *Tracks* are both multivocal narratives, often switching perspectives between different narrators, the narrative forms of the two novels are also quite different. Whereas *Love Medicine* presents an almost dizzying array of narrators and characters, *Tracks* presents the competing voices of just two narrators, the consummate trickster old man Nanapush and the unreliable, undesirable Pauline Puyat. The many voices of Erdrich's narratives complicate popular, oversimplified images of Native Americans and their history. The differences as well as the similarities in the narrative forms of *Love Medicine* and *Tracks* reflect Erdrich's conception of the history of a Chippewa community. If *Love Medicine*'s multivocality expresses the life of a contemporary reservation community, *Tracks* evokes an earlier moment of crisis in that same community's history.

With its shifts between ten different perspectives, including six first-person narrators, *Love Medicine*'s narrative structure expresses a strong and vital community. The various voices and perspectives that make up its chapters emphasize both friction and harmony and place each individual's narrative in the context of a collective, communal narrative. Since Erdrich's narrative structure reflects the dynamics of the community, one might assume that the dual narration of *Tracks* indicates a more unified tribal past than the contemporary contentious atmosphere reflected in the many voices of *Love Medicine*.[23] In fact, the narrators of *Tracks* are more openly hostile to each other's stories (each claiming the other lies) than are any of the narrators in *Love Medicine*, and their philosophical and social differences reflect a community in the grip of spiritual and political crisis.

Tracks chronicles the loss of reservation lands in the early twentieth century despite Fleur's and the others' heroic efforts to save it.[24] Our last view of Fleur in *Tracks* carries her away from her family's land on a road that widens and flattens to "meet with government school, depots, stores, the plotted squares of farms" (*T* 224). Native American critic Gloria Bird accuses *Tracks* of reinforcing traditional stereotypes of the vanishing Indian and accuses Nanapush in particular of romanticism and nostalgia for the past. She quotes Nanapush's description of the passing of the old way of life:

> I guided the last buffalo hunt. I saw the last bear shot. I trapped the last beaver with a pelt of more than two years' growth. I spoke aloud the words of the government treaty, and refused to sign the settlement papers that would take away our woods and lake. I axed the last birch that was older than I, and I saved the last Pillager. (*T* 2)

Bird acknowledges that the series of epidemics of which Nanapush tells us at the beginning of the novel is historically correct, but she claims that the emphasis on dying, together with the fact that Nanapush, Fleur, Moses and Pauline are all the "last" of their bloodlines, represents an internalization of oppression (41–42).

Though I agree that Erdrich calls upon and even emphasizes stereotypes in passages such as the one quoted above, I argue that she does so in order to rework them. Rather than reinforce stereotypes of the "Vanishing Red Man," Erdrich's trickster novels directly undercut those stereotypes, transforming a monologic tribal history into a multivocal cite of contention, connection, and possibility. *Tracks* begins with a history of lost loved ones and dwindling bloodlines, but it also chronicles the formation of new families. In a tricksterlike move of transformation, *Tracks* is an intervention in tribal history: it redefines notions of family and shows the survival tactics that enable the emergence of the strong community evident in *Love Medicine*. As Pauline says of the small band fighting to survive a long winter, "They formed a kind of clan, the new made up of bits of the old" (*T* 70). Nanapush "adopts" Fleur by healing her and then adopts Lulu and passes on his name to her. *Tracks* revises not only Euro-American but also, as Pauline's comments suggest, traditional tribal definitions of kinship.[25] Moreover, although Fleur's departure at the end of *Tracks* signals the dissolution of that new family, the dramatic situation of the novel itself gestures toward recovering connections: Nanapush tells his stories to Lulu, Fleur's daughter, who represents the future of the community. Fleur is indeed the "funnel" of tribal history; the one daughter she produces goes on in *Love Medicine* to repopulate the tribe and take her place as a community matriarch. Ironically, the other matriarch of *Love Medicine*, Marie Kashpaw, is the unacknowledged daughter of *Tracks*'s other narrator, Pauline. Taken together as the history of an evolving community, *Tracks* and *Love Medicine* express the stories not of vanishing relics but of intrepid survivors.

The differences in the narrative forms of *Tracks* and *Love Medicine* reflect the linguistic history of the Anishinabe, or Chippewa tribe. Though Erdrich's form derives in part from oral tradition, her novels also participate in a western literary tradition, with her narrators all speaking and writing in English. *Love Medicine*, which spans 1934 to 1984, reflects a time and a community in which nearly all of the characters have been educated in English-speaking schools. Conversely *Tracks*, which spans 1912 to 1924, reflects an earlier stage in the colonization of the Chippewa, when literacy was less common and the Anishinabe language was spoken more frequently. Their knowledge of English places both Nanapush and Pauline in the position of mediators between traditional ways and an encroaching white world. Erdrich's addition of many Anishinabe words to her revised 1993 edition of *Love Medicine* (the largest editorial change to the text outside of the chapter additions) deepens the issue of language loss; the added chapter "Resurrection" deals extensively with Marie's political decision to turn to the old language because she's lost faith in English.

The narratives of Nanapush and Pauline represent two opposed responses to early twentieth-century Anglo education: Pauline's acceptance of the self-hatred and the confusion of internalized racism and Nanapush's trickster strategies of escape, transformation, and healing humor. Calling himself "a holdout" for the old ways, Nanapush "ran back to the woods" after his Jesuit education (*T* 33), and his wily, witty narratives attest to his faith and pride in Chippewa traditions (despite his constantly overstepping them). Pauline, in contrast, begs her father to send her to the "white town" because "I wanted to be like my grandfather, pure Canadian. That was because even as a child I saw that to hang back was to perish. I saw through the eyes of the world outside of us" (*T* 14). Pauline's increasing madness during the course of *Tracks* grows in large part from this internalized racism, which causes her to reject her Chippewa heritage in a futile grasp for acceptance in a world that scorns her. Susan Perez-Castillo notes that in *Tracks* "the reader shuttles between, not two different perceptions of reality, but two diametrically different realities; that of a people in the grip of disease, death, and spiritual despair, and that of a group of courageous and irreverent survivors" (294). That Erdrich would choose to split *Tracks*'s narrative structure along these lines indicates the centrality of this conflict in Chippewa community history.

As a representation of two opposed realities, *Tracks*'s narrative structure replicates the myth of Chippewa trickster Nanabozho and the great gambler, which we have seen repeated over and over in Erdrich's novels.[26] The competing realities evident in Nanapush's and Pauline's narratives recast an ancient battle over the spirit of the tribe. In his bout with the gambler, the trickster "stopped evil for a moment in a game" (Vizenor, "People" 6). If Pauline's voice represents spiritual despair, then Nanapush's presence in the novel represents a tricksterlike comic challenge to that despair.[27] Nanapush's description of Fleur's laughter at one of the novel's low points captures both the pain and the strength to bond that laughter can express: "rich, knowing, an invitation full of sadness and pleasure I could not help but join in" (*T* 214). According to Nanapush, Fleur is a powerful culture hero; Pauline, in contrast, views Fleur as a misguided throwback. Fleur's insistence on a world in which people would "know better" than to try to buy and sell spirit-filled Pillager land does indeed situate her in the past, but her own mythic strength enables her to reap revenge as she summons the wind to flatten the forest around her cabin, pinning the loggers and their horses (*T* 175).

That nearly all critics of *Tracks* treat the book as if Nanapush is the hero and the main character, and that the book begins and ends with his voice, speaks strongly for Nanapush's success in the battle over the Chippewas' spirit. Nanapush wages his battles with stories.[28] Nanapush muses, "Only looking back is there a pattern. . . . There is a story to it the way there is a story to all, never visible while it is happening. Only after, when an old man sits dreaming and talking in his chair, the design springs clear" (*T* 33–34). Storytelling, by his definition, is analogous to history: both involve the ordering of experience from a retrospective vantage point. Pauline's tricksterlike comment that the story "comes up different every time, and has no ending, no beginning" reminds us that stories, and "objective" history itself, change with every telling and every teller (*T* 31).

Erdrich clearly values the changeability of narrative in her own storytelling process; she uses Pauline's description of storytelling in *Tracks*'s dedication to her husband-collaborator, Michael Dorris.[29] She also connects her own storytelling to Native American and, specifically, Chippewa tradition and history, crediting Gerry Nanapush as trickster in *Love Medicine* as part of that storytelling tradition (Bonetti 90). Speaking of herself and her husband, who is a mixed-blood Navajo, Erdrich says, "When both of us look backward . . . we see and are devoted to telling about the lines of people that we see stretching back, breaking, surviving, somehow, somehow, and incredibly, culminating in somebody who can tell a story" (Bonetti 98).[30] The link between storytelling and survival is vital for Erdrich: it is through the storytelling of her characters that she asserts the survival of Chippewa culture. *Tracks*'s consummate talker old man Nanapush survives by storytelling, which saves his life after consumption has wiped out his family: "I saved myself by starting a story," he says. "I got well by talking. Death could not get a word in edgewise, grew discouraged, and traveled on" (*T* 46). Later, when he nearly freezes and starves to death, "it was my own voice convinced me I was alive" (*T* 7). Like *China Men*'s Bak Goong, Nanapush recreates himself through words. By telling his story—to himself, to Lulu, and to the reader—he recreates his own history, builds a new community, and reconfirms an ongoing cultural tradition.

Erdrich's works embody the trickster's changeability: the stories contain contradictory and alternative truths; they go past their

boundaries as characters move from one book to another, inter-
connect, and converse with one another even between novels. We
learn for instance in *Tracks* that, contrary to what Lulu tells us in
Love Medicine, Fleur did not send her away as a punishment for
playing near a dead body (*T* 218). Moreover, whereas Nanapush
remembers Lulu's homecoming at the end of *Tracks* as his and
Margaret's bracing together "like creaking oaks" to meet Lulu, in
Love Medicine Lulu herself remembers it quite differently: "Nanapush was waiting for me at the crossroads. . . . When the haze
cleared, I also noticed his wife, Margaret Kashpaw. She stood reluctant by his side. Staring at me, her eyes turned to blue-black
metal. Her lips hardened, mean, and her face became a wedge of
steel" (*T* 226; *LM* 69). Though Nanapush's memory reveals an
idealized vision of his new "family," Lulu remains suspicious and
embittered toward Margaret. Since Lulu is Nanapush's explicit
audience in *Tracks*, her own description of the event in *Love Medicine*, told at a later date, clearly revises his.

The fluidity of the trickster's identity and the oral storytelling
process naturally resists the fixity of the printed word. "Nanapush
is a name that loses power every time that it is written and stored
in a government file," Nanapush tells us.[31] Perhaps the best example of Erdrich's effort to preserve the changeability of oral
storytelling is the publication of her new edition of *Love Medicine*.
The notion that even after its 1984 publication the novel re-
mained "unfinished" and revisable destabilizes the assumption of
the permanence of published text. The 1993 version, which adds
four chapters and a large section to one earlier chapter, enhances
many trickster aspects of the novel. The changes reinforce a sense
of dialogue between *Love Medicine* and *Tracks* by weaving more
connections between the two. Not only do we see Lulu's inter-

pretation of the ending of *Tracks*, but Fleur, Nanapush, Margaret, and Moses—all major characters of *Tracks*—make new appearances in the 1993 *Love Medicine*.[32]

The new *Love Medicine* notably expands the stories of two important trickster characters, Lulu and her son Lyman. Lyman's increased presence establishes him firmly as one who forecasts the trickster's role in the future of the reservation community. Though his self-concept is weak, fashioned "out of papers," Lyman voices an alternative perspective on many of the cultural issues that the original *Love Medicine* introduces. Most important, he provides a counterpoint to *Love Medicine*'s other young trickster, Lipsha, and undercuts our previous impressions of characters we thought we knew, enabling us to see them in a more comical light.

Lyman's complete absorption of the values of American consumer culture informs his view of Lipsha: "Slouched in a corner chair away from the table, feet big in unlaced shoes shapeless as plaster, skinny otherwise, wearing a jean jacket cuffed too short for his knobby wrists, he looked puzzled. People treated him special, as though he were important somehow, but I couldn't see it" (*LM* 304). Readers already familiar with Lipsha are likely to be startled by this frank dismissal of him according to common standards of dress and demeanor. Because Lyman has absorbed the dominant culture's values so completely, his observations force readers who share the values of American consumerism to critically reexamine their own perspectives and standards of judgment. Lyman deflates the stature of *Love Medicine*'s central figures and its central values of community and culture building. Yet acidic as his words are, Lyman continues to fulfill the trickster's function by keeping us on our toes, unsettling our comfortable views of favorite characters and reminding us of yet another perspective within this Chippewa community.

Finally, just as Nanapush's stories told to Lulu serve as a pivotal link between *Love Medicine* and *Tracks*, Lyman's two narratives at the end of *Love Medicine* connect that novel to *The Bingo Palace* and suggest the future direction of the community. Through Lyman's vision of a vast bingo hall, which he builds in *The Bingo Palace*, Erdrich again associates trickster strategies to the history of a changing Chippewa community; casinos, a recent and growing phenomenon on Chippewa and many other Native American reservations, are the trickster's newest (and oldest) trick: "Gambling fit into the old traditions, chance was kind of an old-time thing. [Lyman] remembered watching people in a pow-wow tent, playing at the hand games, an old-time guessing event. Casino without electricity. Just hands and songs and spells. . . . Jazz these hand games up with lights and clinkers and you put in shag carpet and you got a Chippewa casino" (*LM* 326–327). Though Erdrich's attitude toward the casinos is ambivalent (Lyman ominously predicts a future "based on greed and luck"), she emphasizes the subversive power of trickster strategies, as Lyman envisions a way to save himself and his community through smooth talk and tricks: "He'd . . . teach Chippewas the right ways, the proper ways, the polite ways, to take money from retired white people who had farmed Indian hunting grounds, worked Indian jobs, lived high while their neighbors lived low, looked down or never noticed who was starving, who was lost" (*LM* 327). Like Gerry's escapes from prison and Fleur's leveling the forest to pin the loggers, Lyman's plan to trick white farmers out of their money overturns the hierarchies. Yet again, as in the great gambler myth, the trickster prevails "for a moment in a game" (Vizenor, "People" 6).

CHANCE AND DESIGN: *THE BINGO PALACE*

With its emphasis on strategy and luck, *The Bingo Palace* invokes the trickster more overtly than any other Erdrich novel and implies the trickster's centrality to contemporary community life. In *The Bingo Palace*, Erdrich plays with the possibilities of chance in narrative structure and community history, acting as trickster author in her orchestration of chance and design—from the characters' elaborate plans to the novel's own layout. The trickster's delight in "narrative chance" allows Erdrich to explore the future of a Chippewa community without containing or prescribing that future.[33]

Unlike the dueling narrators of *Tracks* or the many-voiced narration in *Love Medicine*, the narrative perspective in *The Bingo Palace* poises between individual perception and a group consciousness that emerges as the voice of communal history. Lipsha Morrissey is the novel's predominant (and only first-person) narrator, though he narrates less than half of the novel's twenty-seven chapters and his point of view is interspersed with that of eight others, including an innovative chorus.[34] Lipsha's "I" is balanced most notably by the choral "we," which narrates four chapters, including the book's opening and closing segments. Partly the voice of gossip, the chorus is a (momentarily) unified communal voice that seems to have absorbed the tetralogy's previous three novels: it remarks about Lipsha's failures that "we wish we could report back different since he last told his story" (*BP* 7). In addition, the choral "we" implicitly links the chorus to the reader: "We don't know how it will work out, come to pass, which is why we watch so hard, all of us alike, one arguing voice. We do know that no one gets wise enough to really understand the heart of another, though it is the task of our life to try" (*BP* 6). The chorus's watching is analogous to reading. We might in fact look at reading (or writing) stories as an extension of gossip, of that curiosity we all have in others' lives. By keeping the stories going, the chorus keeps the community alive with its "one arguing voice," a phrase that suggests both unity and multiplicity.

Lipsha's role as trickster in *The Bingo Palace* emerges directly in relation to the choral voice, which defines the community by describing everything Lipsha is not:

> He was not a tribal council honcho, not a powwow organizer, not a medic in the cop's car in the parking lot. . . . He was not a member of a drum group, not a singer, not a candy-bar seller. Not a little old Cree lady with a scarf tied under her chin, a thin pocketbook in her lap, and a wax cup of coke, not one of us. He was not a fancy dancer with a mirror on his head and bobbing porcupine-hair roach, not a traditional. . . . He was not our grandfather, either, with the face like clean old-time chewed leather, who prayed over the microphone, head bowed. He was not even one of those gathered at the soda machines outside the doors, the ones who wouldn't go into the warm and grassy air because of being too drunk or too much in love or just bashful. He was not the Chippewa with rings pierced in her nose or the old aunt with water dripping through her fingers or the announcer with a ragged face and a drift of plumes on his indoor hat. (*BP* 9)

Like Morrison's *Sula*, Lipsha defines the community by his difference. As trickster, Lipsha fits nowhere in this community, yet his central narrative role suggests his importance to the community's future. As a narrative extension of *Tracks* and *Love Medicine*, *The Bingo Palace*'s mix of private and communal perspectives suggests a strong, vital, and unified (if arguing) community.

Lipsha shares his trickster role in *The Bingo Palace* with his uncle Lyman. The struggle between the two forms a pivotal tension in the book. As Lipsha remarks, their relationship, like his relationship to his heritage, cannot be sorted into separate strands of love and hate, jealousy and admiration. "Our history is a twisted rope and I hold on to it even as I saw against the knots" (*BP* 99). The novel's plot revolves around the two men and the one woman they both want, and a parallel struggle between preserving the land in traditional ways and selling out for a money-making casino project. Lyman is a classic trickster who always mixes his own selfishness with the good of the group: "a dark-minded schemer, a bitter yet shaman-pleasant entrepreneur who skipped money from behind the ears of uncle Sam, who joked to pull the wool down, who carved up this reservation the way his blood father Nector Kashpaw did, who had his own interest so mingled with his people's that he couldn't tell his personal ambition from the pride of the Kashpaws" (*BP* 5). As the tribe's leading entrepreneur, Lyman becomes a trickster creator whose plans can "bring the possibilities into existence" and generate badly needed revenue and jobs. Yet, sucked in by his own greed, he gambles away the tribe's loan money and his father's sacred pipe on his first night at a Las Vegas gaming convention, thereby threatening his community's future and traditions. As Nanabozho's struggle with the great gambler reminds us, the trickster's gambles can mean life or death for the community.

Lipsha's awareness of a new crisis facing the Chippewas, the challenge posed by casino gambling, forces him to consider with whom the spiritual future of the tribe lies. Although he senses his own role as the community's next healer and cultural guardian after Fleur Pillager, Lipsha wonders to himself if Lyman might be a more appropriate choice as Fleur's descendant: "Fleur Pillager is a poker sharp, along with her other medicines. She wants a bigger catch, a fish that knows how to steal the bait, a clever operator who can use the luck that temporary loopholes in the law bring to Indians for higher causes, steady advances" (*BP* 221). Despite the novel's repeated insistence on the inconstancy and fluidity of money, a "clever operator" like Lyman may be just what the tribe needs. Lipsha explains that the sides of casino debate are not clear cut: "It's more or less a gray area of tense negotiations. It's not completely one way or another, tradition against the bingo. You have to stay alive to keep your tradition alive and working" (*BP* 221).[35]

As in *Tracks*, the community's survival balances on a dispute over land, and again it is that land most sacred and vital to Chippewa traditions—Fleur's plot on the edge of Lake Matchimanito. "Everybody knows bingo money is not based on solid ground," Lipsha comments, yet despite its shiftiness, gambling is often a viable and necessary way of staying alive and maintaining ground (*BP* 221). After all, in *Tracks* Fleur earned enough money playing poker to temporarily save her land, and in *The Bingo Palace* we learn she has won back the land she lost at the end of *Tracks* in another poker game (*BP* 145). By the end of *The Bingo Palace*, any attempt at human control over land is clearly futile; Fleur's land eventually goes to Lyman's development scheme. "Land is the only thing that lasts life to life," warns Nanapush in *Tracks*, an edict echoed by Fleur in *The Bingo Palace* (*T* 33; *BP* 148). The land itself becomes the ultimate trickster in *The Bingo Palace*, lasting life to life and resisting human efforts to contain, order, and divide it. Just as Shawnee Ray reminds Lyman and Lipsha that she is not theirs to argue over, the land itself reminds them that it cannot be owned but will always slip from their grasp. As the skunk says to Lipsha in a vision, "This ain't real estate" (*BP* 200). The land's permanence reminds us of human impermanence, and the frailty of our attempts to own the land. Lipsha muses,

> Sky, field, and the signs of human attempts to alter same so small and unimportant and forgettable as you whiz by. . . . Passing shelter belts and fields that divide the world into squares, I always think of the chaos underneath. The signs and boundaries and markers on the surface are laid out strict, so recent that they make me remember how little time has passed since everything was high grass, taller than we stand, thicker, with no end. (*BP* 234)

Like the trickster's balance of chance and design, the land's underlying chaos and power is just barely contained under fragile, human-imposed structure.

The trickster's power lies in disruption of pattern, in an ability to negotiate between the known and the inchoate, reminding us that all human design is arbitrary. In *The Bingo Palace*, Erdrich constantly reiterates the interplay between chance and design, both in her characters' attempts to control their own lives and self-referentially in her own narrative structure. The novel is full of intricate plans, from Lulu's "small act" of sending Gerry's picture to Lipsha, which hides a "complicated motive and a larger story" (3), to the "house of pulled strings" that Lipsha imagines Zelda constructing for those around her (14), to Shawnee Ray's elaborate patterns and designs fashioned to bring her independence. Yet although the thought of such human control is appealing, Erdrich emphasizes its drawbacks: in the grip of a heart attack Zelda realizes she has wasted her life, and Shawnee Ray nearly loses her son in her ambition to win a dance competition.

Far from advocating random chance and chaos, however, Erdrich acknowledges maneuverability among the forces of fate. Between chance and design, chaos and order, the trickster operates. From his solitary jail cell, trickster Gerry Nanapush voices the novel's central dynamic: "He knew from sitting in the still eye of chance that fate was not random. . . . Chance was patterns of a stranger complexity than we could name, but predictable. There was no such thing as a complete lack of order, only a design so vast it seemed unrepetitive up close, that is, until . . . one day, just maybe, you caught a wider glimpse" (*BP* 226). Granted an authorlike perspective on the plot of his own life, Gerry senses his participation in a larger design, a feeling reiterated by Lipsha: "I will always be the subject of a plan greater than myself" (*BP* 21).

Although the book suggests design, Erdrich does not enclose plot or characters within that design. Rather, the plot of *The Bingo Palace* permits and even insists on chance and uncertainty. The novel, and the tetralogy, ends not with closure but with possibility. With the most ambiguous ending of the four novels, *The Bingo Palace* never resolves whether it is right or wrong to build the casino; Shawnee Ray, for the moment, chooses neither Lipsha nor Lyman; Gerry has apparently raced off with June's ghost, as the snow erases natural landmarks and finally obliterates boundaries between the living and the dead; Lipsha is left freezing to death (or not) with a baby in a stolen white car; and Fleur seems to have taken Lipsha's place on the road to death, and yet she "still walks," reminding others of her presence (*BP* 273). Fleur, as the tribe's history and its future, leaves her tracks on the snow, a gesture that links the saga's historically oldest and most recent books. Even after death, Fleur watches over the community from the lake: "We believe she follows our hands with her underwater eyes as we deal the cards on green baize, as we drown our past in love of chance, as our money collects, as we set fires and make personal wars over what to do with its weight, as we go forward into our own unsteady hopes" (*BP* 274). The novel ends in characteristic trickster fashion. Fleur's role as trickster at the end of *The Bingo Palace* reminds us of the uncontainability of her culture, of her history, and finally, of what the human mind can understand. Her bear's laugh can be heard on clear nights, but "no matter how we strain to decipher the sound it never quite makes sense, never relieves our certainty or our suspicion that there is more to be told, more than we know, more than can be caught in the sieve of our thinking" (*BP* 274). In *The Bingo Palace*, Fleur becomes the ghost in the machine, the fluid spirit, chance, chaos in the margins of our ordered minds that flashes out, in the novel's last words, "when we call our lives to question" (*BP* 274).

◎

"The trickster's constant chatterings and antics remind us that life is endlessly narrative, prolific and openended," writes William Hynes, and Erdrich's trickster novels express just that ("Inconclusive Conclusions" 212). As Alan Velie reminds us, the trickster is "a figure created by the tribe as a whole, not an individual author" (131), and consequently every trickster narrative revises or comments upon the ones that have come before it, as Lipsha's journey to discover his parentage recasts the Nanabozho origin myth. The trickster could not exist without the community: he or she lives and breathes through stories told and retold and embodies the vulnerabilities and the strengths of the culture. The many voices of Erdrich's novels create life, community, and history through storytelling and express contemporary history in all of its complexity. Central to that history, and inspiring the life of the community, of Chippewa culture, and of Erdrich's narratives, is the trickster. Like Fleur's bear laugh, Erdrich's novels leave us with the sense that there is "more to be told, more than we know, more than can be caught in the sieve of our thinking."

CHAPTER FOUR

Tar and Feathers

Community and the Outcast in Toni Morrison's Trickster Novels

America is a land of masking jokers.
Ralph Ellison, Shadow and Act

That Toni Morrison centers her 1981 novel *Tar Baby* on perhaps the best-known African American trickster tale speaks for the trickster's ongoing relevance in a contemporary world and for the value Morrison finds in trickster strategies. However, the trickster operates much more pervasively in Morrison's work than her contemporary retelling of one popular trickster tale might suggest. Morrison's interest in the trickster stems from her larger interest in the dynamics and the history of African American communities. The trickster, whose fluidity and rule breaking define and maintain culture, embodies a central paradox in Morrison's work: that of balancing the urge to maintain and foster cultural tradition and the equally powerful urge to rebel against its strictures. In her novels, the trickster—as character and as a part of novel form—helps to preserve, define, and defend community while constantly violating its confines.

The trickster is one of the most enduring figures of African American folklore, on which, as Trudier Harris observes, much of African American literature draws: "In a country where, as late as the 1830s, there were laws prohibiting the teaching of slaves, it was necessary for the oral tradition to carry the values the group considered significant. . . . Thematic folk expression and folk beliefs had their parallels in the structural patterns that later shaped the literature" (2). Though folk elements have played a role in African American literature from its beginnings, appearing in works by Charles Chesnutt, Langston Hughes, Jean Toomer, Zora Neale Hurston, and many others, folklore takes on a life of its own in Morrison's work. Rather than include isolated items of folklore, Morrison shows us the process by which folklore is created, transforming historic folk materials into a new folk-based literature (Harris 6).[1]

Br'er Rabbit's position as trickster in African American folklore and culture is a highly controversial one because he is often maligned as a sneaking, selfish, greedy dissembler. Unlike most Native American tricksters, Br'er Rabbit lacks sacred power; in this respect he reflects slaveholders' suppression of African religious practices (Roberts 34). Yet even without sacred status, and despite his dubious reputation, Br'er Rabbit retains mythic power, inspires listeners, and builds culture. Though tales of his antics continue to be told to children as examples of unacceptable behavior (as with Native American trickster tales), Br'er Rabbit's wit, humor, and unfailing ability to survive in a world where the odds are overwhelmingly stacked against him make him tremendously appealing. Br'er Rabbit by no means wins every test of wits; but whether he wins or loses a particular conflict matters less than the accumulated tradition of tales in which he somehow always escapes and survives.[2] The attributes for which the trickster is often condemned—selfishness, slyness, trickery, and an apparent lack of moral sense—were essential adaptive behaviors for enslaved Africans in America. Br'er Rabbit's tricks to secure food, shelter, or his life by duping more powerful animals or Master John made him a folk hero whose behavior became a model for survival (Roberts 29). As John Roberts explains, African and African American tricksters have always been folk heroes: "Enslaved Africans . . . found in their social relationship to and material and physical treatment by the slavemasters sufficient justification for . . . [presenting] the animal trickster as folk hero" (34). Although Br'er Rabbit tales often specifically address the conditions of slavery, Roger Abrahams emphasizes that the African American trickster did not develop simply as a reaction to white oppression; rather, "as in Africa, Trickster's vitality and inventiveness are valued for their own sake" (20).

Br'er Rabbit's tremendous wit highlights an important aspect in African American cultural identity. Because the American slave system involved living with whites in daily power-based relationships, African American trickster tales strongly reflect the necessity for the trickster's subversive, masking, signifying skills. Maintaining any sort of cultural identity under slavery demanded an overt acceptance of, and covert resistance to, the dehumanizing racial myths of slavery. As Houston Baker explains, "A concern for metalevels, rather than tangible products, is . . . a founding condition of Afro-American intellectual history. Africans uprooted from ancestral soil, stripped of material culture, and victimized by brutal contact with various European nations were compelled not only to maintain their cultural heritage at a *meta* (as opposed to a material) level, but also to apprehend the operative metaphysics of various alien cultures" (139). Awareness of coexisting, contradictory versions of reality and an ability to operate and express one's identity at a "metalevel"—primary trickster skills—became a key to survival for Africans in America. Viewed in this light, the multiplicity of worldviews that the trickster embodies and that the works of African American writers such as Toni Morrison express becomes in itself a political statement, a form of resistance and survival.

Perhaps because of the central role women have always played in maintaining African American cultural tradition, Morrison centers her exploration of tricksters and community on women. From Sula to Pilate to Jadine to Beloved, Morrison's work shows a recurring preoccupation with female iconoclasts, wanderers, adventurers, and drifters.[3] Although these women seem an unlikely grouping—Pilate is almost universally praised, Jadine is condemned by critics, and Sula remains an enigma—each woman is a trickster whose highly fraught relationship to her community forms a central concern in the text. With each successive novel, Morrison develops the trickster's relationship to community. *Sula* examines the structure of human community itself, chronicling the life and death not only of one individual but also of the community that defines itself against her iconoclasm. *Song of Solomon* furthers Morrison's exploration of the trickster with the visionary Pilate, who stands at the ideological center of that text. Pilate combines Afrocentric, communal values with the trickster's freedom and fluidity, blurring the traditional African American images of male trickster and female conjurer to question and expand traditionally gendered folk roles. Finally, by explicitly evoking a trickster tale in *Tar Baby*, Morrison uses Son's and Jadine's competing versions of tricksterism to foreground issues of cultural preservation, ancestry, and rootedness. Viewed in terms of competing trickster strategies, *Tar Baby* becomes not merely a condemnation of a wayward daughter but a shrewd deconstruction of stereotyped gender roles. Men and women, this trickster text argues, are equally free to experiment with personal identity and equally responsible for preserving culture.

The trickster's paradoxical, conflicted relationship to community and its challenge to any unified perspective illuminate both the thematic concerns and the structure of Morrison's works. With her trickster aesthetic, Morrison undercuts the possibility of essentializing definitions by race, class, or gender. Tricksters Sula, Son, Jadine, Therese, and Pilate shatter the myth of a definitive "black man" or "black woman"; the trickster's many guises—shape-shifter, charmer, escape artist, magical word-weaver, and conjurer—remind us of the multiplicity of human perspectives. In addition, the trickster operates on a structural and linguistic level in her novels, embodying her wandering, multidimensional point of view and her use of masking and signifying to disrupt and create meaning. The trickster's ability to express multiple and conflicting possibilities, her or his talent for engaging an audience on various levels, points toward the political and aesthetic aims of Morrison's art: challenge, provocation, and engagement.

TRICKSTER AS ICONOCLAST: *SULA*

Sula's iconoclasm, her complete disregard for societal values, suggests her affinities to the trickster. Trudier Harris has noted Sula's resemblance to Br'er Rabbit, who "is independent in a world where community cooperation is the norm; he frequently acts against the wishes of the community or takes advantage of their work. . . . [H]e does as he pleases, guided by what suits him rather than by any communally accepted ethical system" (71). Though we might expect such a figure to pose a threat to community, Morrison shows us that in fact Sula sustains and gives life to her community by giving them a reason to unite. Although the novel's title implies that Sula is the book's central character, *Sula*'s structure belies that center by foregrounding the community.[4] The novel opens with the elegy of a community soon to be razed entirely by the swing of a wrecking ball. Sula herself is not mentioned for another two chapters, which cover two years and introduce Shadrack (the community's sanctioned outcast) and Nel (its individuated representative).[5] Neither does the book end with Sula's death; two chapters and twenty-five pages follow her demise. The novel's layered structure highlights the levels on which Sula's behavior and indeed her very existence inform the community's life.

In the inverted world of the Bottom, Morrison defines a specifically nonwestern cosmology, of which Sula, as trickster, forms a vital part. "He was not the God of three faces they sang about. They knew quite well that he had a fourth, and that the fourth explained Sula" (*S* 118).[6] Sula's "evil" ways actually make the community stronger, as they unite against her as pariah. "Once the source of their personal misfortune was identified, they had leave to protect and love one another. They began to cherish their husbands and wives, protect their children, repair their homes and in general band together against the devil in their midst" (*S* 118). Ironically the trickster's presence inspires the community toward positive trickster survival strategies: "The presence of evil was something to be first recognized, then dealt with, survived, outwitted, and triumphed over" (*S* 118). Sula does not embody pure evil in the traditional religious sense, but rather she exists outside of a dichotomized good and evil. She is not immoral but amoral, and the trickster's amorality sharpens the community's sense of a moral code. By constantly violating societal norms, Sula paradoxically helps to define the social fabric.[7]

That Sula holds community together becomes abundantly clear at her death, which also signifies the death of the community:

> A falling away, a dislocation was taking place. Hard on the heels of the general relief that Sula's death brought a restless irritability took hold. . . . Mothers who had defended their children from Sula's malevolence (or who had defended their positions as mothers from Sula's scorn for the role) now had nothing to rub up against. The tension was gone and so was the reason for the effort they had made. Without her mockery, affection for others sank into flaccid disrepair. (*S* 153)

The community's response to Sula highlights the anarchic trickster's crucial role in maintaining a system of social relations. Trickster creates the tension that upholds the society's structures. Without Sula's scorn to "rub up against," even motherhood becomes meaningless.

The community's disintegration culminates on the National Suicide Day after Sula's death, when Shadrack unwittingly leads a huge crowd to their icy death as they move in an enraged mass to destroy the tunnel they were forbidden to build because of racist labor practices. The tunnel collapses, and many suffocate and drown (*S* 161). After Sula's death, the community has deteriorated to the point where its people form mobs and commit suicide—acts that Morrison had earlier insisted were beneath them.

Sula's ambiguous birthmark, the rose-tadpole-knife-copperhead over her eye, marks her as a trickster, as does her unrestricted sexuality—the comedy, irony, and outrage she feels in "lying under someone, in a position of surrender, feeling her own aiding strength and limitless power" (*S* 123). Her attitude toward the transaction of sex suggests how Sula, as trickster, helps to create a social world. As Robert Pelton writes of the Ashanti trickster Anansi, in all social dealings the trickster

> embodies transaction. For this reason he is a mediator
> specializing in "exchanges"—a perpetually open passageway.
> He transforms by no plan except the shape of his own urge
> to realize the act of dealing, yet because this drive necessarily
> creates intercourse, he establishes the social geography of
> the world in the very process of playing out his own inner
> design. (225)

Thus Sula "establishes the social geography" of the novel with her iconoclastic behavior.

Like the trickster, Sula enacts the taboo and lives the desires others are ashamed to admit they have (Nel recollects years later her own pleasure at watching Chicken Little's fingers slip from Sula's hands). Sula recognizes no common morality and no social boundaries, asks people rude questions, and more dramatically, sleeps with her best friend's husband without a second thought. Even Sula's death questions the boundaries of life. True to her trickster's sense of comedy, her own death makes her smile as she experiences no break in consciousness but a freedom from physical responsibility: "'Well, I'll be damned,' she thought, 'it didn't even hurt'" (*S* 149).

Although Sula's character clearly contains many trickster elements, she lacks the ego and sense of purpose (even for selfish gains) that most tricksters have. Two things have pushed Sula outside the human community: her mother's casual remark that she loves but doesn't like her, and Chicken Little's accidental(?) death. "The first experience taught her there was no other that you could count on; the second that there was no self to count on either. . . . She was completely free of ambition, with no affection for money, property or things, no greed, no desire to command attention or compliments—no ego. For that reason she felt no compulsion to verify herself—be consistent with herself" (*S* 119). Such selflessness creates a freedom analogous to the trickster's, but the trickster is often motivated by greed, ambition, or social reputation. Sula's freedom is perhaps more terrifying for its lack of reference to any other human being. Sula leads an "experimental life" and functions in the novel as an experiment in character that goes beyond traditional trickster traits (*S* 118). With Sula, Morrison shows both how a "bad" trickster can be "good" for the community and how far the mythic trickster's amorality and disorder can apply to the human character. In other words, Sula shows both the power and the limits of a trickster positionality for real human beings: the freedoms it affords and the ultimate costs it demands.[8]

Sula's disconnection from the social fabric associates her with sources of creativity, making her a potential visionary and suggesting a reason for Morrison's experiment with her. Morrison implicitly aligns Sula's position with her own as creative artist by calling Sula an "artist with no art form": "had she paints, or clay, or knew the discipline of dance, or strings [or writing, we might add]; had she anything to engage her tremendous curiosity and her gift for metaphor, she might have exchanged the restlessness and preoccupation with whim for an activity that provided her with all she yearned for" (*S* 121). Sula's friendship with Nel, the one sustained connection of her life, disintegrates because Nel cannot stand the disconnection from community. Unlike Nel, whose dependence on society makes her "one of the spiders whose only thought was the next rung of the web," Sula chooses a "free fall" from society's web: "that required—demanded—invention." Outside of the social web, in her rich, creative, dizzying free fall, Sula sees "the slant of life that made it possible to stretch it to its limits" (*S* 120). Though Sula is a failed visionary, her free fall from the social web allows Morrison to view that web on the slant. As a trickster who transforms by challenging her community and a visionary whose human limitations cannot survive her own mythic power, Sula stretches the bonds of human community to their limits. We cannot, finally, judge Sula's life, because she refutes any and all value systems on which we might base judgment. Sula is perhaps most like the trickster in her resistance to critical evaluation. Likewise, in resisting our analysis, Morrison's literary experiment with *Sula* works: the trickster once again eludes interpretation.

COMMUNAL TRICKSTER: *SONG OF SOLOMON*

Like Sula, *Song of Solomon*'s mythical Pilate is an outlaw and a wanderer, unwilling to sustain a long-term relationship with a man, oblivious to many of society's norms, and just barely tolerated on the outskirts of her community. Yet Pilate combines the trickster's freedom and fluidity with a deep commitment to personal relationships, which makes her Morrison's strongest, most visionary female trickster. "She is like something we wish existed," Morrison comments. "She represents some hope in all of us" (McKay, "Interview" 416). With Pilate, Morrison builds on Sula's iconoclasm to reinvent the trickster: rather than simply an agent who disrupts and creates social order, in Pilate the trickster becomes a strong source of personal and communal identity.

Despite Pilate's singularity, however, many feminist critics have found fault with *Song of Solomon* for its foregrounding of Milkman's rather than Pilate's story. Cynthia Davis writes, "When the time comes to fulfill the myth, to show a hero who goes beyond the independence to engagement, she creates a male hero" (19). Likewise, Trudier Harris notes that "on the landscape of Morrison's fictive imagination, women stand only with the assistance of men, but men grow over the deranged or dead bodies of women" (190), and Barbara Christian observes that Pilate "derives her accumulated wisdom from her father and primarily benefits Milkman, her nephew, rather than any other woman in the novel" ("Trajectories" 243).

Yet to read Pilate's role as secondary to Milkman's merely because he fulfills a quest is to privilege a value system that Morrison by no means endorses. Milkman's quest indicates his incomplete identity, in contrast to Pilate's wholeness. "I chose a man to make that journey because I thought he had more to learn than a woman would have," Morrison comments (McKay, "Interview" 428). Significantly, the author describes her use of the quest motif in *Song of Solomon* as "my own giggle (in Afro-American terms) of the proto-myth of the journey to manhood" ("Unspeakable"

29). That Morrison "giggles" in *Song of Solomon* at one of the most powerful and pervasive western myths, that of the solitary male quest for identity, signifying on it to question and subvert its power, considerably alters our view of the quest motif in the novel. "Whenever characters are cloaked in Western fable," Morrison says of her own work, "they are deep in trouble" ("Unspeakable" 29). Viewed in light of a nonwestern tradition, Milkman's heroism diminishes in stature, whereas the importance of seemingly secondary characters such as Pilate expands. Morrison explains, in fact, that Pilate's apparently secondary role in the novel results ironically from her fear that Pilate might "take the book over": "She was a very large character and loomed very large in the book. So I wouldn't let her say too much" (McKay, "Interview" 416).

Pilate's great power derives from her ability to combine the trickster's freedom and fluidity with a strong connection to community. Her metamorphosis at the police station from a tall, imposing figure to a diminutive shuffling old woman reminds us of Gerry Nanapush's magical abilities and has prompted several critics to identify her as a trickster.[9] But Pilate's tricksterlike qualities extend far beyond a single incident. She approaches androgyny in her balance of "the best of that which is female and the best of that which is male" (Morrison, "Rootedness" 344). Morrison confesses rather guiltily in one interview that black men's freedom to "split," to disengage from family and community responsibilities, "has always been to me one of the most attractive features of black male life. I guess I'm not supposed to say that. But the fact that they would split in a minute just delights me" (Stepto 392). Pilate combines the culture-building qualities associated with women with the male trickster's freedom to "split."

As Carolyn Denard observes, Pilate's "values are like those of all tar women: a caring concern for home, family and community" (175).[10] Yet a close look at her life requires a dramatic redefinition of terms like *home* and *family*. Before her daughter is born, and from the time Reba is two, Pilate leads a "wandering life," settling down only when she discovers that her "prissy" granddaughter Hagar needs "family, people," and the "prosperous, conventional" life she had long ago rejected (*SOS* 148, 151). With no street address, no furniture, and no electricity, Pilate's eventual home offers little in the way of conventional comforts. Yet the spiritual comfort of this home affords Milkman the first "completely happy" moment of his life, and a glimpse into their candlelit home spellbinds even the materialistic Macon Dead (*SOS* 47, 29). Pilate's rejection of modern conveniences has led some readers to dismiss her as an appealing but impractical throwback.[11] However, Pilate's history of repeated rejections makes it clear that she does not merely belong to a more communal agrarian past but has in fact always been "apart." Like *Tracks*'s Fleur Pillager, whose relationship with the water god Missepeshu set her at a distance since childhood, Pilate's lack of a navel indicates her supernatural and transformative power. For both women, rejection of modernity indicates not so much a stubborn clinging to the past as an assertion of tricksterlike otherness, an otherness that relies on violating conventions.

In Pilate's unconventional home, Morrison balances the community and continuity that she associates with women and the freedom and wanderlust that she associates with men. Pilate's profession of producing and selling bootlegged liquor expresses the balance of nurturer and outlaw; although she supports herself by trafficking an illegal substance, she neither drinks nor allows her customers to consume their goods on her property (*SOS* 47). However, Morrison carefully distinguishes between Pilate's strengths as a culture bearer and ancestor and the traditional values of motherhood: neither Reba nor Hagar achieves the stature or self-reliance of their mother and grandmother, perhaps partly because of their indulged and fatherless childhood. Attributing Reba and Hagar's weaknesses in part to the absence of men in their lives, Morrison emphasizes that Pilate herself had a close, loving family in her father and brother until she was twelve. Yet although Morrison suggests that Pilate has spoiled Hagar, she is careful to limit a mother's responsibility for her children: "Strength of character is not something one can give another," she comments (McKay, "Interview" 419). Morrison's aim is not to glorify Pilate as a mother figure but to include motherhood as one aspect of her wide-ranging identity.

Several critics have noted Pilate's importance as a communal figure.[12] As her wandering life suggests, however, Pilate's relationship to community is hardly traditional: she is, from the young Milkman's perspective, the "ugly, dirty, poor, and drunk . . . queer aunt whom his sixth-grade school mates teased him about" (*SOS* 37). Rule breaker and perpetual outsider within the community, Pilate functions as a communal trickster in the novel. Though Pilate follows none of society's rules, giving up, for example, "all interest in table manners or hygiene," she defines its most essential values in her "deep concern for and about human relationships" (*SOS* 150).

Pilate's sign of difference, her smooth stomach with no navel, which terrifies men and women and isolates her from all permanent human contact, signals her connection to the sacred. Pelton's discussion of tricksters as uniting the sacred and the profane describes Pilate: "They help found their people's modes of life and mediate between gods and men precisely because 'trickiness' unites sacrality and profanity. . . . The trickster's doubleness becomes both the source of his transforming power and the reason for his banishment from the community; as profaner of the sacred he becomes a sacred being, yet remains an outsider, the victim of his own violations" (245). Pilate's access to the spiritual world and its sacred powers alienates her; the first group of migrants she joins regard her smooth stomach with pity and terror, rejecting her as something that "God never made" (*SOS* 144).[13] Having birthed herself, inching her way out of her dead mother's body, Pilate escapes the normal ties of aging and death and has special access to the spiritual world, speaking to the dead and concocting potent salves and solutions to create and protect Ruth's baby.[14]

Pilate's negotiating ability, rootworking skills, and connection to a spiritual world identify her as a conjurer, as Joseph Skerrett among others has noted (Skerrett 195). Despite the stereotype that conjurers were hated and feared as practicers of evil witchcraft (a western bias to which Macon Dead, for one, fully subscribes [*SOS* 54]), conjurers were the repositories of African religious systems (Roberts 68). John Roberts usefully illuminates the role of the conjurer as "that of a trickster possessed with spiritual power" (103). The conjurer as developed under slavery, Roberts explains, maintained group harmony by controlling destructive trickster behavior within the community (102–103). The trickster's role in relation to community varies widely, as the differences between Sula and Pilate suggest. Trickster behaviors that betray the community, like Sula's disregard for marital bonds and Jadine's rejection of her family and culture in *Tar Baby*, are dangerous and resented. Morrison comments, "My work bears witness and suggests who the outlaws were, who survived and why, what was legal in the community as opposed to what was legal outside it" (LeClair 371). Tricksters are outlaws and survivors, whose actions, depending on where they are directed, help to either preserve or destroy community.

Pilate's role as a communally centered conjurer, perhaps the most powerful of culture-building trickster figures, accounts for the unequivocally positive view of the trickster that she embodies, in contrast to the more conflicted views of tricksters in *Tar Baby*.[15] When the story involves a black community and an external, oppressive power, the trickster's role becomes more problematic, since it depends upon whites accepting and perhaps believing in the outward mask. Maskers risk reinforcing oppressive stereotypes in order to maneuver behind them.[16] Pilate's trickster role within the community provides a much more important and powerful model for community and cultural strength than does any of the interracial trickster maneuvering in *Tar Baby*. In fact, the one time that Pilate acts the conventional trickster role in the white world, she provokes Milkman's intense shame and discomfort:

> Nothing was like the shame he felt as he watched and listened to Pilate. Not just her Aunt Jemima act, but the fact that she was both adept at it and willing to do it—for him . . . opening herself wide for their amusement, their pity, their scorn, their mockery, their disbelief, their meanness, their whimsy, their annoyance, their power, their anger, their boredom—whatever would be useful to her and to himself. (*SOS* 211).

Milkman's shame, though inspired partly by his own bad behavior, reveals his, and Morrison's, deep ambiguity toward the use of masking strategies when dealing with whites.

Finally, the visionary Pilate shares Morrison's tricksterlike storytelling talent. She models her stories on the needs of the moment, making even her life story "deliberately long to keep Ruth's mind off Hagar" (*SOS* 152). Pilate's storytelling connects her to the role of the traditional African griot, a teaching storyteller who guards cultural traditions.[17] Pilate's life example, as a free, whole person who creates home and community without being tied to any of their conventional trappings, makes her a truly visionary figure. Yet although Pilate is certainly an important teacher for Milkman, Morrison emphasizes Pilate's lack of access to her own family's past. Her comical misunderstanding of her father's injunction to "Sing" (really a revelation of her mother's name) and not to "fly off and leave a body" (a reference to the story's central myth of the flying Africans, which she misinterprets as a command to retrieve a murdered man's bones) sets Pilate up as a trickster who both instructs and is duped.

TRICKSTERS IN CONFLICT: *TAR BABY*

In *Tar Baby*, Morrison introduces her most elaborately developed array of trickster characters, whose conflicting attitudes toward community allow her to simultaneously affirm the importance of culture building and challenge prescribed gender roles within African American communities. In her 1981 preface to *Tar Baby*, Morrison explains that she did not "retell" the story: "I fondled it, scratched and pressed it with my fingertips as one does the head and spine of a favorite cat—to get at the secret of its structure without disturbing its mystery."[18] This approach suggests a view of the folktale as a dynamic, living entity, which responds to but is never fully controlled in the hands of its storytellers.

As one of the best-known and most widely told of Br'er Rabbit's adventures, the tar baby tale has appeared in countless contexts—from its traditional African antecedents, to Joel Chandler Harris's plantation frame, to a Disney movie (Werner 155). Though historical change and the specific context of each telling inevitably frame the folktale along differing lines, Morrison's *Tar Baby* does not merely produce another version of the tale. Morrison herself emphasizes that she did not read any version of the tale before writing the novel; she relied on her own memory rather than "trust the literature and the sociology of other people to help me know the truth of my own cultural sources" ("Memory" 386). In *Tar Baby*, Morrison explores the tale's provocative and paradoxical implications in order to suggest the trickster's visionary, culture-building potential.

The novel's title invites comparison to the tar baby tale. Briefly, the tale involves a farmer (or sometimes Br'er Bear) who sets a "tar baby" by the side of the road to trap Br'er Rabbit. In many, but not all versions, the tar baby is specifically gendered as female. When Br'er Rabbit passes by, he greets the tar baby, who does not respond; angered, Br'er Rabbit swats at her repeatedly until he is completely affixed to the tar. While the farmer deliberates over an appropriate punishment, the trickster begs him to do anything but throw him in the briar patch, which the farmer, of course, immediately does. Br'er Rabbit laughingly escapes, calling out that the briar patch is his home.[19] The tale highlights Br'er Rabbit's recognition and manipulation of the farmer's cruelty and blindness. It also emphasizes that Br'er Rabbit can be duped by illusion but that he ultimately saves himself by remembering his "home," or cultural roots.

Much criticism of the novel has focused on Morrison's use of the tale, particularly as it plays out in the relationship between Son and Jadine.[20] Son quickly emerges as the outlaw thief who gets "stuck on" the European-educated, western-formed "tar baby" Jadine. This identification made, however, the permutations of the tar baby story in the novel become convoluted: though Son displays many of the trickster's features, Jadine also displays some; moreover, each must struggle against the adhesive, entrapping "tar" of the other, and each envisions a very different briar patch, or safe home. The struggle between them becomes a struggle over African American culture, waged through competing gendered images of the trickster and competing cultural values associated with tar. Additionally, Morrison includes a third trickster, the mythical, visionary, and apparently marginalized Therese. A blind seer, Therese disrupts the polarity of the Son-Jadine conflict, challenges the limits of western perception, and affirms the primacy of ancestral roots to communal identity through her connection to the island's mythical swamp or tar women.

Son, certainly, is the classic trickster, a nameless outlaw, a masterful storyteller, a catalyst whose presence disrupts the tenuously held serenity of the social order. Son's fluidity allows him to manage "a face for everybody" and a different story for each circumstance (*TB* 142, 143). Like Br'er Rabbit in the farmer's garden, Son hides and steals food scraps where he can, drinking bottled Evian in a modern variation on the traditional well water of the tale. Like Gerry Nanapush, *Love Medicine*'s modern Nanabozho, the outlaw Son uses his trickster capabilities to avoid imprisonment: "In eight years he'd had seven documented identities and before that a few undocumented ones, so he barely remembered his real original name himself. Actually the name most truly his wasn't on any of the Social Security cards, union dues cards, discharge papers, and everybody who knew it or remembered it in connection with him could very well be dead. Son." Son as trickster exists outside of conventional social roles, and his name in this context implies both relationship and disconnection. Morrison links Son to an "international legion" of wanderers whom we might call modern tricksters and thus suggests a contemporary world in which tricksters abound. Son is part of a social phenomenon generated by the need, for various reasons, to escape the confines of conventional life:

> day laborers and musclemen, gamblers and sidewalk
> merchants, migrants, unlicensed crewmen on ships with
> volatile cargo, part-time mercenaries, full-time gigolos, or
> curbside musicians. What distinguished them from other
> men (aside from their terror of Social Security cards and
> *cedula de identidad*) was their refusal to equate work with life
> and an inability to stay anywhere for long. . . . Anarchic,
> wandering, they read about their hometowns in the pages
> of out-of-town newspapers. (*TB* 142–143)

This lengthy, romantic description of contemporary tricksters pays tribute to such wanderers and reclaims the forgotten and marginalized as an important part of a larger community. It also suggests Morrison's attraction to the fluidity of identity and the promise of adventure that such an "anarchic" life affords.

Like the trickster who moves in all worlds, Son crosses boundaries easily. In borrowed suits and silk pajamas, he moves effortlessly from Valerian, the rich white employer who calls Gideon

"Yardman," to Therese, the mystic islander who refuses to even "acknowledge the presence of the white Americans in her world" (*TB* 94). Son's dealings with people of all social levels heighten our sense of both the insurmountability and the flimsiness of social boundaries.

Son and Jadine's radically different perspectives on New York highlight how Morrison complicates the notion of the "briar patch," the safe home into which the farmer unwittingly throws Br'er Rabbit as punishment in the tar baby tale. "Of the two views of the Briar Patch, the farmer's and the rabbit's, which was right?" Morrison asks (Preface i). Whereas Jadine feels that "if ever there was a black woman's town, New York was it," Son senses "silent and veiled" crying in New York (*TB* 191, 185). The city functions as a terrifying trap to Son but as a safe, liberating briar patch to Jadine, whereas Son's own briar patch, the sleepy town of Eloe, Florida, frightens Jadine as much as New York horrifies Son. The traditional tar baby story, Roberts observes, warns against "accepting illusion for reality" and reminds one to "always remember one's cultural roots" (42). As the shifting images of the briar patch in *Tar Baby* imply, all safety may be an illusion, and one's cultural roots depend greatly on how one locates and defines culture. In the struggle over African American values, the conflict between Son and Jadine represents two ultimately unbridgeable perspectives: "One had a past, the other a future and each one bore the culture to save the race in his hands. Mama-spoiled black man, will you mature with me? Culture-bearing black woman, whose culture are you bearing?" (*TB* 232). Morrison's refusal to resolve this dilemma has led at least one critic to pronounce the book "a failure" (Coleman 73). Yet, just as a traditional African storyteller uses a tale not to provide solutions or pass judgment but to explore a dilemma, Morrison uses Jadine, and indeed all of *Tar Baby*, not to solve a cultural problem but to suggest "what the conflicts are" ("Rootedness" 341). Morrison's trickster strategy in *Tar Baby* is not to provide solutions to the opposed perspectives of Son and Jadine but to show the limits of each totalizing view. Morrison does not attempt to weave together Son's and Jadine's two opposed social webs; rather, recalling Sula's "free fall" from the web, she shows us their limits and, in so doing, demands invention and opens new possibilities (*S* 120).

With an art history degree and a modeling career, Jadine is Morrison's most materially successful black female character and, many argue, her least sympathetic.[21] Jadine rejects the communal values that Morrison esteems so highly, and she has been lambasted by critics as selfish, hollow, and even "the embodiment in language of the carcinogenic disease eating away at the ancestral spirit of the race" (Traylor 146). Yet if we view Jadine as Morrison's exploration of the gendered and cultural implications of the tar baby tale, we begin to appreciate the value she holds for Morrison. In her novelistic revision of the tar baby tale, Morrison critiques not only white stereotypes of blacks but also the entrapping sexism inherent in the nostalgic myths of black women. As both tar baby and trickster, Jadine presents a challenge to essentializing views of the tar baby and to the different standards applied to male and female tricksters.

Morrison's treatment of Jadine as tar baby demonstrates her boldly revisionist view of the story. The trickster's power in the tar baby tale lies in manipulating the farmer's control over him, in inverting his powerlessness into subversion. By questioning the tar baby's motives and emphasizing the positive as well as the negative qualities of tar, Morrison undercuts or subverts any monologic message in the tale. Morrison approached the tar baby tale with several key questions: "Why does the tar baby cooperate with the farmer, and do the things the farmer wishes to protect wish to be protected? What makes his job more important than the rabbit's, and why does he believe that a briar patch is sufficient punishment, and what does the briar patch represent to the rabbit, to the tar baby, and to the farmer?" (Preface i). Morrison's questions assume that the tar baby has autonomy, will, and thoughts of its own. This is a crucial revision of the traditional tar baby tale, in which the master creates the tar baby as an unspeaking object whose "essence" is definable and understandable to others. By radically questioning this restrictive view of the tar baby, and by complicating the meaning of tar itself, Morrison makes an essentialized view of Jadine, or any character, extremely difficult.

The contrast between the trickster's freedom of movement and the dense, adhesive quality of tar forms a central tension in the tar baby story. Jadine's ambiguous relationship to tar allows Morrison to examine all of its connotations and to explore Jadine as both tar baby and trickster. Her scary encounter with tar early in the novel aptly captures this duality, as Jadine sinks up to her knees in a swamp of pitch. Like the tar baby of the tale, she waits, covered with tar, by the side of the road for Son. Her angry silence on their trip home echoes the tar baby's silence, and like Br'er Rabbit who swats at the tar baby for her rudeness, Son becomes even further enmeshed in his affection for Jadine (*TB* 158).

However, because Jadine is not an object but a subject, we witness her outrage and terror at being covered with tar and labeled a "tar baby." Her struggle with its tenacious embrace reveals a deeper struggle with aspects of her own identity, culture, and heritage. In the swamp scene, Morrison specifically associates the mythical tree women who watch Jadine struggling below them with the highly ambiguous properties of tar:

> They were delighted when they first saw her, thinking a runaway child had been restored to them. But upon looking closer they saw differently. This girl was fighting to get away from them. The women hanging from the trees were quiet now, but arrogant—mindful as they were of their value, their exceptional femaleness; knowing as they did that the first world of the world had been built with their sacred properties; that they alone could hold together the stones of the pyramids and the rushes of Moses' crib; knowing their steady consistency, their pace of glaciers, their permanent embrace, they wondered at the girl's desperate struggle down below to be free, to be something other than they were. (*TB* 157)

The tree women's "sacred properties" are those of tar: the "steady consistency" and the adhesiveness that build and maintain pyramids and cultures. Morrison explains that for her, "the tar baby came to mean the black woman who can hold things together" (LeClair 373). The positive connotations of tar in the novel derive from a combination of the tar lady of African mythology, the historic sacredness of the tar pit, and the use of tar as a building material (LeClair 373). In this context, Jadine's desire to break free and to define herself differently appears unnatural and unwomanly.

Yet, in the context of Morrison's other female tricksters, Jadine cannot be read merely as the tarred outcast of Morrison's fictional community, since we know the outcast's inherent power as a visionary who sees beyond the limits of society's confining web. If on one level Morrison highly values tar as an image of the strength of black women, she also sympathizes with Jadine's urge to flee. To a young, active, independent African American woman like Jadine, the tree women's "steady consistency, their pace of glaciers, their permanent embrace" represent stagnation and death (*TB* 157). Jadine's tarring in the swamp plasters her with a fixed definition of black womanhood, which threatens her own subjectivity. During her stifling nights in Eloe, she dreams of motherly night women who threaten to "grab the person she had worked hard to become and choke it off with their soft loose tits" (*TB* 225). The night women, like the ladies behind the church basement pie tables in Son's daydreams, represent a trap to Jadine (*TB* 3). Morrison's maternal imagery, so often a source of cultural strength in her novels, appears suffocating and threatening here. Although Jadine no more represents a model for communally responsible behavior than does Sula, her aversion to traditionally accepted women's roles opens up new possibilities for an identity unrestricted by gender. From the moment Jadine begins her struggle to disengage from restrictive definitions of black womanhood, she embodies not just the tar baby but also the trickster.[22]

By escaping the confining, tarlike strictures of community and responsibility, Jadine embodies a tricksterlike survival that Morrison cannot wholly condemn. If Son runs like Br'er Rabbit into the woods at the end of *Tar Baby*, "Lickety-split, lickety-split, lickety-lickety-lickety split," Jadine also "splits" at the end of the novel, escaping not only from Son but also from the reader's view by "making tracks" on a plane to Paris (*TB* 243). Jadine's vow to return to Paris and "begin at Go," reinventing herself, strongly echoes powerful trickster Pilate's decision to throw away "every assumption she had learned and beg[i]n at Zero"—an echo that bodes well for Jadine's survival and success (*SOS* 149).

That the freedom to "split" has long been associated with men may help to explain why Jadine's behavior attracts such virulent criticism. Trudier Harris suggests that "we would readily accept all that Jadine is, and most of her actions, if the doer of the action were male instead of female. In other words, African-American folk culture has not prepared us well for a female outlaw, or for a beauty queen with the traits of an outlaw" (128). Curiously, Harris herself links Jadine's role as trickster to a specifically female seductive power and emphasizes Jadine's affinity to the Indian and African "trickster/tempter who has the potential to bring about the downfall of the men she encounters" (13). Yet although Son refers to Jadine as a "tar baby side-of-the-road whore trap," Morrison's attitude toward a female trickster does not divide so easily along reductive gender lines. Son holds his position as a communal folk trickster in a modern world because he can wander freely while sustaining nostalgic memories of "yellow houses with white doors which women opened and shouted Come on in, you honey you! and the fat black ladies in white dresses minding the pie table in the basement of the church" (*TB* 102). Son's gendered daydreams in no way threaten his own male freedom. In contrast, Jadine, into whom Son attempts to "press" these dreams, is necessarily confined by images that place her behind pie tables and in houses and church basements. As a female iconoclast, Jadine shatters gender barriers and tastes that delightful "male" freedom. If Morrison highly values the adhesive, "steady consistency" of tar, and the communal strength it represents, she equally values the tricksterlike urge in both men and women to escape its trappings.

As if to forestall any new definition of "the" female trickster, Morrison counterbalances Jadine's tricksterlike impulse away from communal responsibilities and strictures with the community-based trickster Therese. Much like Pilate, whose apparently marginalized role as Milkman's guide places her at the center of the novel's value system, Therese transcends her position on the borders of the Son-and-Jadine conflict in *Tar Baby*, as her non-western ways of knowing challenge every assumption on which Isle des Chevaliers society is built. As spiritual guide for Son and laundry maid for the Streets, Therese is far closer to the tree women than to the girl struggling to escape from them. Discredited within her own community as a blind, foolish old woman and written off by her employers as a faceless "Mary," Therese wields remarkable power within the narrative to remind us that "discredited knowledge," in Morrison's terms, is valid and powerful ("Rootedness" 342).

With her nephew Gideon, Therese reenacts a traditional Br'er Rabbit adventure when they try to steal apples from the Streets's pantry—not because they are starving, but because Therese has always craved apples (*TB* 93). Though Valerian Street brutally plays his role as the farmer by firing both Gideon and Therese, Morrison undercuts the severity of the consequences for these tricksters by depicting an island "briar patch" that amply makes up for their expulsion from the Streets's "garden." Unlike the rich and middle classes who depend on wilted, spoiled imports, the poor "ate splendidly from their gardens, from the sea and from the avocado trees that grew by the side of the road" (*TB* 93). The islanders play on the arrogant ignorance of their employers: Gideon pretends illiteracy to avoid extra work, and Therese, fired many times, counts on her employers' blindness and keeps returning as the "new" girl. A seer gifted with second sight to compensate for her blindness, Therese sees Son in a dream and recognizes his ties to the mythic blind, naked horsemen that roam the island (*TB* 89). Immediately sensing Son's starving presence on the island, she begins to leave him food; she creates a secret, subversive community under the noses of her employers (*TB* 90).

Like Son, Therese shares the trickster's fluid storytelling talent. She invents scenarios of passion and betrayal among the house's inhabitants:

> "And machete-hair she don't like it. Tried to keep them apart. But it didn't work. He find her, swim the whole ocean big, till he find her, eh?" . . . The more she invented the more she rocked and the more she rocked the more her English crumbled till finally it became dust in her mouth stopping the flow of her imagination and she spat it out altogether and let the story shimmer through the clear cascade of the French of Dominique. (*TB* 92)

By refusing to translate the "clear cascade" of Therese's island French, Morrison reminds readers of the limits of their own access to certain kinds of knowledge, allowing us in this case to appreciate Therese's storytelling skill while withholding her story. Also in French, Therese's "thirty-four letters in fifteen years" trick Gideon into returning to the island to "take care of the property by which she must have meant herself because when he got there that's all there was left: no land, no hills of coffee bush" (*TB* 92).

Morrison employs Therese as a trickster character to throw the edges of differing perspectives into sharp relief. She emphasizes the limits of others' perspectives by exploring Therese's "complex and passionate" hatreds, and she also highlights Therese's own limited perspective by noting that Therese has left the whites out of her story: "She had forgotten the white Americans. How would they fit into the story? She could not imagine them" (*TB* 95). Therese's inability to imagine whites results from her daily refusal "even to acknowledge the presence of the white Americans in her world" (*TB* 94). She stares vacantly when they come within view, so that, as Morrison comments, "what they took for inattentiveness was actually a miracle of concentration" (*TB* 95). Therese's willful blindness to whites expresses her contempt for their presence and their power and recalls the mythic blind horsemen who survive free on the island by virtue of their blindness.

Though a survival tactic, Therese's blindness mirrors the whites' (and even Sydney's and Ondine's) blindness to her. In all cases, Morrison suggests, such willed or unconscious obtuseness is limiting. Just as the Streets's blindness allows Therese, Gideon, and Son to trick them, Therese's blindness limits her storytelling power. Therese realizes that "all her life she thought [whites] felt nothing at all. Oh, well, yes, she knew they talked and laughed and died and had babies. But she had never attached any feeling to any of it" (*TB* 95). This objectification echoes and inverts a familiar rationale for slavery and suggests the damaging results of colonization on Isle des Chevaliers: dominance breeds its own infection in others. By suggesting the ease with which a refusal to admit other perspectives can become a rationale for dehumanizing others, Morrison exposes the danger of willed ignorance.[23]

A blind seer, Therese heightens our awareness of the intersections between worlds. Her access to the mythic world of the horsemen allows her to perform one of the trickster's most important functions: like the iconoclastic Sula, Therese finds a way of "extracting choice from choicelessness," giving Son a chance at the end of the novel to join the mythic horsemen or to go back to Jadine (Morrison, "Unspeakable" 25). By tricking him into landing on the back side of the island, Therese creates new possibilities for Son and changes what seemed a prescribed, choiceless situation to produce dialogue, ambiguity, and chance. Though Gideon and others mock Therese, Morrison takes every opportunity to validate her and the "discredited knowledge" of folklore and myth that she represents ("Rootedness" 342). In Therese's powder pink house in the hills, Son gains his first sense of community, comfort, and belonging: "He stretched his legs and permitted himself a hearthside feeling, comfortable and free of postures and phony accents" (*TB* 129). Moreover, as Peter Erickson observes, the novel grants "Therese power to realize her vision" in the end, as nature seems to guide Son into the forest to join the horsemen (303). Significantly, Morrison chooses Therese to echo the novel's dedication to women who "knew their true and ancient properties": "She has forgotten her ancient properties," Therese says of Jadine (*TB* 263). Like Erdrich's repetition of *Tracks*'s dedication in Pauline's words, Morrison chooses her most discredited speaker to revoice the words of her novel's dedication. In doing so, both authors validate traditionally discounted viewpoints. Although Morrison's dedication appears to validate Therese at the expense of Jadine, the conflict between them is no more resolved than is any other conflict in *Tar Baby*. Rather, Morrison presents Jadine's and Therese's competing versions of female tricksterism to suggest a range of possible trickster behaviors available to women. Clearly, Morrison esteems the communal values that Therese represents, but she by no means offers up Therese's life as an ideal. Herself a highly successful black woman, Morrison is suspicious of the stultifying images of black women that tend to accompany invocations of communal values, as suggested by Son's dreams of welcoming pie women and Jadine's dreams of smothering mothers. By presenting versions of the trickster in Jadine and Therese, Morrison celebrates both Therese's mysterious, mythic, tar-woman power and Jadine's freedom to escape and reinvent herself.

Morrison finally presents many more questions and possibilities in *Tar Baby* than she does solutions. The novel's ending leaves the reader with a heightened awareness of the borders of different worldviews and the sense of fragmentation that such awareness brings. To readers and critics expecting resolution, cohesion, and closure, *Tar Baby*'s ambiguous ending appears frustrating and unsatisfying. Yet if we view the novel's ending in the context of its ongoing concern with shifting meanings and perspectives, the ending's refusal to settle the fundamental questions it raises makes it consonant with the trickster tale tradition on which it draws. African American trickster tales, as Roger Abrahams observes, are always "to be continued" (3). Morrison specifically connects *Tar Baby*'s ending to an African dilemma tale tradition, distinguishing it from western folktales "where they all drop dead or live happily ever after" (Darling 6). Looking for that kind of closure is unrealistic, Morrison suggests; even if the trickster escapes this time, he or she may not the next (Harris 207). As the novel closes with narrow escapes, missed connections, and unresolved possibilities, one might imagine Morrison executing her final trick on any reader still expecting a conventional marriage ending. Like the listeners of dilemma tales, readers must work through the text's contradictions and come up with their own solutions. By sparking debate among readers and critics about "ancient properties" and individual freedom, Morrison helps to transform the society she represents, one deeply divided along race, class, and gender lines.

"PURE TRICKSTER POETICS": MORRISON'S NARRATIVE STRUCTURE

The most successful and visionary trickster of Morrison's novels is Morrison herself. Joseph Skerrett's description of trickster Pilate underscores the similarities between the singer of Solomon's song and the author of *Song of Solomon:* "Pilate is the frightening source of uncomfortable questions and liberating truths. . . . Pilate is isolated but loving, reaching out to those in need of her knowledge. But she also requires her students to come up to the lesson, to enter into the act of communication" (19). Just as Pilate asks uncomfortable questions within the story, Morrison asks uncomfortable questions on a narrative level, employing trickster strategies in constructing her novel. In raising these questions, revealing liberating truths through the trickster techniques of masking and signifying, and reaching out to those in need of her knowledge, Morrison creates a communal art form and demands that her readers "come up to the lesson" and "enter into the act of communication" (Skerrett 199). Morrison's trickster aesthetic can perhaps best be captured in her own description of "what makes a work 'Black'": "The most valuable point of entry into the question of cultural (or racial) distinction, the one most fraught, is its language—its unpoliced, seditious, confrontational, manipulative, inventive, disruptive, masked and unmasking language" ("Unspeakable" 210). In his study *Indi'n Humor*, Kenneth Lincoln aptly calls Morrison's description "pure trickster poetics," and so it is: the trickster operates linguistically to disrupt, unsettle, and create meaning. Houston Baker's identification of the "metalevels" of culture at which "Africans uprooted from ancestral soil" were forced to operate provides one historical explanation for the "masked and unmasking" quality that Morrison characterizes as distinctly African American (136). The ability to maintain culture at any level in the face of negation and erasure requires the trickster's masking, maneuvering, signifying skills. Signifying, which Henry Louis Gates Jr. describes as "the language of trickery," is the linguistic embodiment of the mask (*Signifying Monkey* 54). Signifying language creates a worldview that allows for paradox, contradiction, and multiple perspectives. In calling attention to metalevels of experience, masking or signifying language embodies a trickster aesthetic, which seeks to destabilize absolute perspectives and essentializing definitions. Using language as a mask to signify on accepted meanings allows the speaker a tricksterlike freedom. The mask creates maneuvering room, as Morrison explains: "language, if it is to permit criticism of both rebellion and tradition, must be both indicator and mask, and the tension between the two kinds of language is its release and its power" ("Memory" 389).

Masks work on a linguistic level in *Tar Baby*, in allowing critique of both "rebellion" (represented by Jadine) and "tradition" (represented by Son and the tar women), which reminds us that neither perspective is flawless. Morrison's play on the word *tar* provides a useful example of her signifying technique. Though tar entraps, it also embodies community and culture building, the adhesive that binds human relationships. Moreover, Morrison's elaborate description of the swamp's history deepens the resonance of the tar imagery. Created by an unnatural, colonizing human invasion of the island, the swamp had been a river that "lost its course" in the wake of construction and development: "Evicted from the place where it had lived, and forced into unknown turf, [the river] could not form its pools or waterfalls, and ran every which way . . . until exhausted, ill and grieving, it slowed to a stop just twenty leagues short of the sea" (*TB* 7). Morrison's description of the swamp's origin mirrors the mythic story of the slaves who were struck blind at the sight of the island. The swamp's unappealing aspect makes Jadine avert her eyes "whenever she drove past" because it suggests the unpleasant memory of the island's slave past that Jadine would just as soon forget (*TB* 155). Ironically, in this colonialist context, the tar created by the swamp represents a consistency and stick-to-it-ness necessarily created by slavery.

Morrison's tricksterlike narrative technique recalls Mikhail Bakhtin's description of the origin of narrative point of view. Comparing the novelist's strategy to the trickster's masking, Bakhtin suggests that masking has been a part of the novel from its beginnings:

> the novelist stands in need of some essential formal and
> generic mask that could serve to define the position from
> which he [or she] views life, as well as the position from
> which he [or she] makes that life public. And it is precisely
> here, of course, that the masks of the clown and the fool
> (transformed in various ways) come to the aid of the novelist.
> These masks are not invented: they are rooted deep in the
> folk. (163)

Bakhtin's clown and fool are versions of the trickster, and it is not surprising that in a trickster novel so deeply rooted in folk traditions as Morrison's *Tar Baby*, the trickster's masking techniques define the narrative's texture.

The narrator of *Tar Baby*, like the trickster, is "life's perpetual spy and reflector," who wanders from one character to another peeking beneath or ripping off masks (Bakhtin 161). Morrison's trickster narrator most clearly emerges as the "unsocketed eye . . . adrift and curious" that wanders through the house watching its sleepers, listening in on their dreams, revealing their secrets (*TB* 36). Significantly, this unsocketed narrative eye also materializes in Son, who moves through the house at night, existing in its margins and on its scraps, unknown and undetected, watching its inhabitants (*TB* 51, 102). Approximating the narrator's fluid, constantly shifting perspective with his free and easy movement among the worlds of all of the other characters, trickster protagonist Son embodies the narrative perspective.[24] Bakhtin's description of the liberating power of a masking trickster perspective expresses the dynamics of *Tar Baby:*

> In the struggle against conventions, and against the
> inadequacy of all available life-slots to fit an authentic human
> being, these masks take on an extraordinary significance.
> They grant the right *not* to understand, the right to confuse,
> to tease, to hyperbolize life; the right to parody others
> while talking, the right to not be taken literally, not "to be
> oneself"; . . . the right to rip off masks, the right to rage at
> others . . . —and finally, the right to betray to the public
> a personal life, down to its most private and prurient little
> secrets. (163)

Bakhtin's "right to parody others while talking" and "right not to be taken literally" approximate, in slightly different terms, the linguistic freedom of African American "signifying" that Morrison uses to great extent in *Tar Baby*. Son's "struggle against conventions," his refusal to be labeled, his skill at signifying, and his access to the house's secrets all match Bakhtin's description and embody the novel's tricksterlike narrative perspective.[25]

Though Bakhtin's discussion of the trickster's masking techniques bears usefully on Morrison's work, Morrison's approach to masking differs in at least one significant respect from his. Viewing the mask primarily as a theatrical device, Bakhtin assigns no importance to the features behind the mask, whereas Morrison, aware of a long African American history of masking as a survival strategy in a racist society, emphasizes the mask's interior contours as well as the tensions between the mask and what it conceals ("Unspeakable" 30). As one of the trickster's primary tools, the mask preserves its wearer's perceptive power while hindering that of others.[26] Morrison's comparison of *Tar Baby*'s structure to a mask calls attention both to the space between the mask and the masked, and to the mask's interior and exterior surfaces as inversions of one another. She describes the novel's structure as a "piece of mask sculpture: exaggerated, breathing, just athwart the representational life it displaced. Thus, the first and last sentences had to match, as the exterior planes match the interior, concave ones inside the mask" ("Unspeakable" 30–31). *Tar Baby*'s first sentence, "He believed he was safe," and its last, "Lickety-split, lickety-split, lickety-lickety-lickety split," match and reverse each other, taking us, in Morrison's words, "from a dream of safety to the sound of running feet. The whole mediated world in between" ("Unspeakable" 31). The tensions between the mask and what it hides contain worlds, Morrison suggests, and offer tremendous mediating freedom to tricksters who wear the mask.

However, Morrison's trickster aesthetic encompasses more than masking techniques; it also incorporates a multiplicity of worldviews that include "discredited," nonwestern "ways of knowing" (Morrison, "Rootedness" 342). Robert Pelton's description of West African tricksters Legba, Ogo, and Eshu provides a useful perspective on the trickster as a narrative principle that incorporates multiple perspectives: "All three show their trickiness more by their agility than by their pranks. People may or may not laugh at their wiles, but they know their slipperiness as that of sacred transactors, middlemen whose power lies in their capacity to face every way at once" (226). Morrison narrates not only through the eyes of Son, Jadine, and Therese, but also through those of Gideon, Sydney, Ondine, Valerian, and Margaret, and thus creates a point of view that faces every way at once. Indeed, insofar as her trickster aesthetic includes an awareness of multiple levels of reality, Pelton's discussion of tricksters clarifies Morrison's exploration of the sacred more usefully than does the term *magical realism*.[27] As Pelton explains, the trickster exposes the sacredness of everyday life, "the sacredness that discloses itself when the world is seen to be more than meets the eye, 'something other,' a web of multidimensional planes of being, a Sigui dance where all beings, human and nonhuman, meet and move together in a single pattern" (256). *Tar Baby*'s extensive attention to nonhuman life forms—the terrified champion daisy trees, the "poor insulted, brokenhearted river," and the butterflies scandalized at Jadine's sealskin coat—expresses this aspect of her trickster aesthetic (*TB* 8, 74). Morrison's novel vividly expands our sense of the world as "a web of multidimensional planes of being" (Pelton 256). By presenting so many competing perspectives, Morrison's tricksterlike narrative voice effectively undermines the stability or plausibility of any single point of view, whether it be human, animal, or vegetable.

If, as Pelton suggests, the trickster reveals the world as a "web of multidimensional planes of being," then the orchestration of these planes' intersections, in effect the creation of community through dialogue, defines Morrison's trickster aesthetic. Though critics have noted the importance of community as a theme in Morrison's work, I suggest that it is also a means of ordering the narrative itself. By transforming barriers into connections and enabling exchange and understanding across worlds, the trickster "spells out cosmic designs in human language, . . . opens passageways into all that is still wild, and . . . transforms social boundaries into modes of intercourse" (Pelton 236). The trickster aptly defines *Tar Baby*'s ever-shifting cosmic, communal narrative viewpoint. Despite his or her singularity, the trickster embodies communal art by allowing the individual artist intercourse with and expression of the whole community. As Pelton observes, "It is not autonomy that Legba is after, but intercourse" (247). Morrison clearly views the aims of her art as communal: "If anything I do," she explains, "isn't about the village or the community or about you, then it is not about anything" ("Rootedness" 344).[28] Morrison implicitly connects the reader and the community by linking both to the function of the chorus in her novels, explaining that her use of chorus derives from its function in "Afro-American communal structures" ("Unspeakable" 2). In *Tar Baby* the chorus, which she defines as "the community or the reader at large, commenting on the action as it goes ahead," includes the natural world: butterflies, flowers, and soldier ants. The community of *Tar Baby* extends its nature and scope with a tricksterlike cosmic viewpoint.[29]

With *Tar Baby*, Morrison invents a form that both expresses and creates community, and that community clearly extends beyond the boundaries of the book to engage the reader. Morrison emphasizes reading as participatory; the text functions not as "the authority" but as "the map," a web of crossroads (like Pelton's "web of multidimensional planes of being") that the reader must negotiate (Morrison, "Memory" 389). As she has repeatedly explained, Morrison aims for an oral quality in her work that reinforces the reader's role as one among many listeners ("Rootedness" 341; Christina Davis 418; McKay, "Interview" 427). She explains, in terms that recall Pelton's interactive, communal trickster, that "the language has to have holes and spaces so the reader can come into it. . . . Then we (you, the reader, and I, the author) come together to make this a book" (Tate 125). Rather than supply narrative commentary that instructs readers how to judge the vast array of perspectives she presents, Morrison reserves judgment, insisting that each reader must establish his or her own bearings on the "map" of her text.

Morrison's conception of communal art incorporates the trickster's emphasis on transaction and intercourse and derives from both African and African American cultural forms that emphasize improvisation and audience participation.[30] This communal art also relates to African storytelling traditions, where, as Abrahams explains, "the entire community might be involved in the telling," during which the community "celebrates its identity as a group" (18). *Tar Baby* and *Song of Solomon*, with their ambiguous, signifying endings (Son searches for Jadine and enters the myth; Milkman both dies and flies), unsettle rather than soothe us by supplying questions rather than answers.[31] "I am very happy to hear that my books haunt," Morrison comments: "That is what I work very hard for" (McKay, "Interview" 421).

◎

Morrison's description of Son's choices in *Tar Baby* mirrors the choice and the challenge she offers her readers: "He is determined to live in that briar patch, even though he has the option to stay with [Jadine] and live comfortably, securely, without touching the borders of his life" (Watkins 50). A true trickster, Son pushes his limits and lives intensely, uncomfortably, always "touching the borders of his life." Morrison wonders if Jadine will throw away her dreams of safety and do the same (Watkins 50). If in *Tar Baby* Morrison presents the seemingly insurmountable challenge of reconciling tradition and rebellion, community and individuality, *Song of Solomon*'s visionary Pilate combines the trickster's fluidity with connection, and individuality with exchange. Morrison's trickster aesthetic illuminates and values contradictions, celebrates and affirms community, and involves and unsettles the reader. By encouraging our awareness of the borders of our own perceptions, Morrison's works enhance our tricksterlike perception of a "web of multidimensional planes" of experience in which "all beings, human and nonhuman, meet and move together in a single pattern" (Pelton 256). She also challenges us to the dangerous, exhilarating, inventive "free fall" from that web.

CHAPTER FIVE

Conclusion

When cultures collide, jokes mediate playfully, permitting the differences.

Kenneth Lincoln, Indi'n Humor

Certainly the time frame we presently inhabit has much that is shabby and tricky to offer; and much that needs to be treated with laughter and ironic humor; it is this spirit of the trickster-creator that keeps Indians alive and vital in the face of horror.

Paula Gunn Allen, The Sacred Hoop

Over time, land, and oceans, Nanabozho, Br'er Rabbit, and Monkey wink at each other on the contemporary scene. Maxine Hong Kingston set *Tripmaster Monkey* in the sixties because "Monkey was here, in the Sixties. Abby Hoffman, Allen Ginsberg . . . They were monkey spirits, trying to change the world with costumes and street theater" (M. Chin 61). Over thirty years later, as Paula Gunn Allen's comment suggests, our shabby, tricky world needs trickster more than ever. Humor, Kenneth Lincoln reminds us, is crucial "when cultures collide" (41). Recent novels by contemporary women of color show that Monkey, Nan-abozho, and Br'er Rabbit are flourishing, playfully mediating the cultural collisions of contemporary American culture, and challenging, engaging, and healing us with inventive, visionary novels. The trickster's historical roots in social and political engagement, together with trickster's fluidity of form and transgression of boundaries create a flexible, dynamic, culturally grounded model for reading the novels of contemporary ethnic American women writers. Like its protean inspirer, the trickster aesthetic links fluidity and specificity, individual and community, alienation and intercourse, and substance and form.

Though the works of Kingston, Erdrich, and Morrison all participate in western novelistic traditions, neither the term *postmodern* nor many contemporary feminist approaches adequately describe their works' complex, communal narrative structures or account for the cultural specificity so central to their works. Many novels of contemporary ethnic women writers demand a new critical approach that reflects the diversity—and the specificity—of their worlds. In the case of women of color especially, who for so long have been spoken for rather than listened to, critics would do well to take their cues from the writers themselves and turn to the trickster. The trickster aesthetic, with its postmodern awareness of disjunction, multiplicity, and paradox, and its roots in specific cultural traditions, fulfills the call for such a flexible, inventive, and culturally aware critical approach.

The trickster in each tradition grows out of distinct, historically specific cultural landscapes and traditions that require individual attention. Yet, placing Maxine Hong Kingston, Toni Morrison, and Louise Erdrich in one study points to a major trend in contemporary ethnic women's fiction: the trickster as a key model for identity, cultural discourse, and novel form. As Robert Pelton observes, "The knotty logic of the trickster is best unraveled by keeping him firmly situated within the cultural context. . . . At the same time, looking clearly at the trickster on his home ground would unveil the common, though analogical, imaginative process that shapes him in each culture" (Pelton 18). Though Erdrich, Kingston, and Morrison obviously draw on distinct cultural and historical traditions (Nanabozho, the Monkey King, and Br'er Rabbit share few particularities), the three writers work from a common cultural and historical context—the interconnected, diverse, and often conflicting worlds of contemporary America. For each writer, the trickster embodies the rich paradoxes of inhabiting interconnecting worlds.

Because the trickster, like other folk and mythic figures, develops under specific, constantly evolving cultural conditions, the trickster's importance in literary works has changed over time. Certainly the writers in this study are not the first American ethnic writers to use trickster strategies. But whereas earlier writers— Charles Chesnutt, Sui Sin Far, Mourning Dove, Zitkala-Ša, and Zora Neale Hurston, for example—had to resort to subversive strategies to negotiate a place in American culture, contemporary ethnic writers have more freedom and more say in their own literary production. As Bonnie TuSmith notes, in contemporary texts "tricksterism is as much a conscious artistic technique as it is the result of an oppressive publishing environment" (*All My Relatives* 31). The contemporary trickster operates less by subterfuge than by inspiring open celebration and laughter. Writing tricksters becomes less of a subversive and more of a celebratory culture-building act. As contemporary novels show, the trickster now freely examines the deceptions inherent in the mask, becoming a source of overt outrage and healing laughter as well as a trope for a contested and contesting community. The trickster in contemporary women's writing provides a way of laughing at damaging stereotypes and celebrating culture and community.[1] Moreover, the trickster's humor, polyvalence, and multivocality suggest a valuable mode for interaction on a textual and a personal level in an increasingly complex, multicultural world.

As "sources of community," iconoclastic tricksters paradoxically embody community (Pelton 227). The trickster texts of Morrison, Erdrich, and Kingston express the contemporary conditions of their communities: Morrison's splitting of tricksters Son and Jadine in *Tar Baby* suggests the split she sees in the contemporary African American community; Erdrich's trickster novels express the history of a Chippewa community, from a moment of crisis in the split narration of *Tracks* to the vision of communal strength in the multivocal *Love Medicine;* and Kingston's comic, multivocal *Tripmaster Monkey* looks toward revitalizing a strong Chinese American community by interweaving many more conflicting voices.

Each of these texts allows space for the reader's voice; all three writers, by explicitly involving the reader in the construction of the text, implicitly expand the notion of the community to include non–African Americans, non–Native Americans, or non–Chinese Americans. Yet, even as the texts demand reader involvement, the multivocality of trickster novels does not dilute their cultural specificity. As Robert Pelton reminds us, "It is the trickster, above all, who . . . transforms social boundaries into modes of intercourse" (236). As writing tricksters, Erdrich, Kingston and Morrison transform boundaries into connection points and open "modes of intercourse" through which readers can engage with texts and people can form connections across cultures. Forming community, as these texts make abundantly clear, does not entail molding a monolithic, univocal front that enforces boundaries between those included and those excluded; rather, these works suggest a trickster-based model of community that thrives on multivocality, connection, and exchange.

For the ethnic American women writers in this study, the trickster aesthetic provides both a way into cultural specificity and a means of escape from essentializing definitions. In none of the cultural traditions considered in this study did the trickster originate as a response to white oppression or encroachment.[2] But in Chinese American, Native American, and African American literary traditions, the trickster has become, among other things, a valuable figure for cultural and personal identity in the face of racism and essentializing stereotypes. The trickster's shapeshifting and polyvocality makes him or her a compelling figure not only for cultural resistance and survival but also for blasting images of the monolithic Indian, Black, or Chinese American.

The trickster in contemporary women's texts acts both as a figure of cultural strength and rebellion and as a sign of diversity. The trickster's unity in diversity aptly expresses Toni Morrison's assertion about African Americans, that "the major thing that binds us is the clear identification of what the enemy forces are . . . what separates us are the things that separate all people" (Christina Davis 417). Kenneth Lincoln similarly observes that "Navajo and Sioux and Hopi and Crow and Chippewa aren't much unified on anything but resistance to Anglo encroachment" (22). For contemporary ethnic American women writers, the trickster aesthetic liberates divergent, contesting voices from the need to present a unified front. Without weakening its political vigor, the trickster transforms the novel into a dynamic, provocative site of engagement among all perspectives, including the reader's.

◎

The trickster can never, finally, be defined. As Robert Pelton puts it, trickster has skillfully "slipped out of our contemporary interpretive nets to thumb his nose at both scholarly and popular understanding of so-called primitive peoples. Yet these peoples too know their trickster as the very embodiment of elusiveness" (1). Precisely because trickster cannot be pinned down to any one form, shape, or position and he or she continually disrupts the status quo with laughter, jokes, and outrage, trickster embodies an expansive, dynamic cultural identity rather than a reductive, static one. The resurgence of the trickster on the contemporary literary landscape—especially in novels by women of color—speaks for the figure's importance not only to theme but also to stylistic innovation in the contemporary ethnic novel. Drawing on the "spirit of the trickster-creator," to use Allen's words, Kingston, Erdrich, and Morrison remind us of the trickster's power to laugh at old worlds and invent new ones.

NOTES

CHAPTER ONE

1. For a full articulation of this materialist-feminist viewpoint, see Newton and Rosenfelt's preface to *Feminist Criticism and Social Change*. See also Carby's valuable introduction to *Reconstructing Womanhood*.

2. Radin's classic *The Trickster* relies on a Jungian view of the Winnebago trickster. See also Knapp; and Frye's "Archetypal Criticism" in *Anatomy of Criticism*. Frye insists on "a single pattern of significance, out of which myth constructs a central narrative" for all literature ("The Archetypes of Literature" 93).

3. In this study, the trickster is variously referred to as a figure of "archetype," "myth," and "folklore," according to context. There seems to be no critical agreement about the definitions of these three terms; rather the borders between them shift among and even within cultures, and with each writer. In my view, the urge to define myth, archetype, and folklore as discrete categories is itself a product of a western mindset, one which the writers considered here mean to challenge.

4. The "trickster aesthetic" that I identify refines the "folk aesthetic" that Marilyn Sanders Mobley sees in the works of Toni Morrison and

Sarah Orne Jewett. Mobley notes that "the goal of their art is to redeem or transform their culture through narrative fiction" by reclaiming folklore (*Folk Roots and Mythic Wings* 9). The specific importance of trickster folklore becomes especially clear in the works of women of color.

5. See also TuSmith's valuable study *All My Relatives*, which argues for the centrality of community in all ethnic American texts.

6. The intersection of these two studies helps to explain the common aims of the trickster narratives of women of color. Zagarell focuses predominantly on nineteenth-century literature by white, middle-class women. She notes, but does not explain, two modifications that many twentieth-century writers have made to the narrative of community: the prominence of "folkloric, mythical, occasionally magical elements" and "the fashioning of community, whether political or cultural" as an often explicit objective in twentieth-century narratives of community (527). For women of color, the enhanced emphasis on community-building surely derives from greater perceived threats to their respective cultures than those that nineteenth-century white women would have felt. The myth, folklore, and magical realism of Erdrich, Kingston, and Morrison's works derive from a culture-building objective as well as from a nonwestern, broader sense of the real.

7. See Lauter; and Ostriker.

8. Pratt in fact calls this mythic perspective "phobic" (11). Newton and Rosenfelt note that archetypal feminist criticism tends to disregard the differences among women, positing myths of "female heroes and female quests . . . without as a rule concerning itself with the social conditions that generate or impede the imagining and experiencing of heroism in daily life" (xxxi, n. 7). For a survey of recent American feminist work on myth, see Lauter 9–15.

9. Discussing sexism, for example, King-Kok Cheung notes that "black [female] silences, deepened by the history of slavery, are not the same as Chinese American silences, which were reinforced by anti-Asian immigration laws" ("Don't Tell" 163).

10. For more on this relatively new, culturally aware approach to comparative trickster studies, see Doty and Hynes; and Ammons's introduction to *Tricksterism in Turn-of-the-Century American Literature* (vii–xiii). The chapter epigraph from Yellowman is quoted in Doty and Hynes 29, who cite Barre Toelken, "The 'Pretty Language' of Yellowman: Genre, Mode, and Texture in Navaho Coyote Narratives," *Genre* 2.3 (1969): 221.

11. Among the many tricksters in world literature, Turner lists "the Greek god Hermes, the Norse god Loki, the Yoruba deity Eshu-Elegba, the Fon Legba, the Winnebago trickster Wakdjunkaga, and many others" ("Myth and Symbol" 580). Turner explains that myths "treat of origins but derive from transitions. . . . Myths relate how one state of affairs became another: how an unpeopled world became populated; how chaos became cosmos; how immortals became mortal" ("Myth and Symbol" 576).

12. William Hynes offers a helpful cluster of six characteristics that many tricksters share: "(1) the fundamentally ambiguous and anomalous personality of the trickster. Flowing from this are such other features as (2) deceiver/trick-player, (3) shape-shifter, (4) situation invertor, (5) messenger/imitator of the gods, and (6) sacred/lewd bricoleur" (34).

13. Noting that trickster behavior often goes "against the Western grain," Doty and Hynes observe that "much of American religiosity (whether pop or formal) has trouble with both the comic and the deceitful," the trickster's realm (28). For an excellent discussion of western versus (nonwestern) Kalapalo views of the trickster, see Basso 1–6.

14. See especially Lenz; Lindberg; and Wadlington. For a notable exception to this largely nineteenth-century, white male focus, see Ammons and White-Parks.

15. Lenz suggests that the confidence man, while appearing marginal, actually embodies central aspects of the American character: "The horror at the center of antebellum culture, the cause of the Civil War and the source of the corrupt Gilded Age, is an infinite capacity for

confident self-delusion visible in the history of the confidence man; preaching equality, opportunity, and freedom, society enforces submission to its self-serving, self-destructive conventions. . . . The confidence man is no longer a marginal predator but a national symbol of American culture" (183). Even in the guise of the confidence man, the trickster teaches through dupes and scams.

16. See Lindberg 8.

17. Tricksters did not disappear from American literature in mid-century. Recent critical attention to tricksterism has focused on Ralph Ellison and Flannery O'Connor, among others. See Lindberg's chapter on Ellison; and Johansen.

18. For an excellent history of America's changing literary canons, see A. LaVonne Brown Ruoff and Jerry Ward Jr., eds., *Redefining American Literary History* (New York: MLA, 1990).

19. Simone de Beauvoir made this point in 1952 (xliii).

20. Compare Vizenor's description of the trickster as "liberator," in "Trickster Discourse."

21. See "Discourse in the Novel," especially 400–405, for a more detailed discussion of these three figures. Bakhtin himself does not escape a limited viewpoint; his discussion of social languages in literary forms ignores factors such as gender or ethnicity—elements that nevertheless take part in any speaking position.

22. As Ruthann Knechel Johansen explains, the trickster "makes visible the limitations and artifice of all closed systems" and therefore makes "the reader distrust the absolute authority of the temporal-material world" (11). For further discussion of the trickster's potential for radical vision, see Turner's investigation of the liminal in *The Ritual Process;* and Bakhtin's analysis of the carnivalesque in *Rabelais and His World*, Trans. Helene Iswolsky (Bloomington: Indiana UP, 1984).

23. Karen Oakes notes that Vizenor's own exclusive, academic language weakens his politically radical ideas by making them inaccessible to all but the educated elite (148).

24. In her discussion of Kingston's *Tripmaster Monkey*, Patricia Lin states that "ethnic Americans, by virtue of their hybridized experiences . . . in a sense have always carried the essential germ of the postmodern" (334). See also Kim, foreword xi–xvii.

25. Anzaldúa's description recalls Han Suyin's maintenance of a "boneless coherence" in the face of her multiple identities (Suyin, *Destination Chungking*, as quoted in Ling 115).

26. The Anita Hill and Clarence Thomas hearings provide a vivid recent example.

27. The emphasis on defining identity through connection to one's community, which Gilligan and Nancy Chodorow assert is characteristic of female self definition, is one example of this intersection of "female cultural values."

28. Franchot Ballinger notes that there are "relatively few female tricksters in the Native American tradition, just as there are relatively few female picaros in the European tradition" (36, n.1) Andrew Wiget comments that the predominance of male tricksters may, at least in the Native American tradition, result from the bias of male ethnographers, who "expected elder males to be the repository of traditional knowledge and seldom sought out women storytellers" (89).

29. See note 10.

30. I am indebted to Ann Detmer for her observations in an unpublished paper on Vizenor's view of the trickster.

31. See Dasenbrock for a treatment of the differing reading strategies of readers who share or do not share the writer's ethnic background.

32. See Bauer 4.

33. TuSmith's discussion of "literary tricksterism" has obvious similarities to my concept of a "trickster aesthetic," many of which I discuss in my chapter on Kingston. I am indebted to TuSmith's identification of ambiguity as a positive trickster strategy, both in the working out of identity and in connecting oral to written form. My concept of a "trickster aesthetic" expands on TuSmith's ideas in including a focus on

multivocal narrative structure, actual trickster characters, and the social and political implications of "tricksterism."

34. Giovanni's comment recalls Maxine's remark to her mother in *The Woman Warrior* on learning they've lost their land in China: "Now we can live anywhere, Mama. We belong to the planet now" (*WW* 107).

35. This between-world perspective also includes other marginalized groups, such as gays and lesbians.

36. bell hooks notes the surprise she felt in her first Women's Studies class at Stanford: "White women were revelling in the joy of being together—to them it was an important, momentous occasion. I had not known a life where women had not been together, where women had not helped, protected, and loved one another deeply" (*Feminist Theory* 11). See her *Feminist Theory from Margin to Center*, for an extensive treatment of this topic.

CHAPTER TWO

1. Although Ling is referring in this passage specifically to Chinese immigrant women, Kingston, as a second-generation Chinese American brought up by immigrant parents, would have faced many of the same cultural taboos.

2. Indeed, these signs have prompted at least one critic to characterize Kingston's technique in *The Woman Warrior* as "literary tricksterism." See TuSmith's valuable chapter on Kingston in *All My Relatives* for a discussion of Kingston's use of ambiguity as a narrative strategy employed to explore her own ambivalence and to capture orality in writing.

3. See, for example, Hunt; and Woo.

4. For a full exploration of Kingston's destabilization of rigid definitions, see Schueller.

5. For two excellent reviews of the male-female debate that *The Woman Warrior* has occasioned, see Lee; and Cheung, "The Woman Warrior versus the Chinaman Pacific."

6. Kingston's extensive re-visioning of the traditional Chinese legends of Fa Mu Lan and Ts'ai Yen constitutes another aspect of her trickster strategy, a technique that I explore more fully in my discussion of *Tripmaster Monkey*. Kingston's tampering with traditional myths in *The Woman Warrior* has been well documented. See especially Schueller; S. Wong; Cheung, "Don't Tell"; TuSmith, "Literary Tricksterism"; and Li, "Naming."

7. In the text, *The Woman Warrior* will be cited parenthetically as *WW*, *China Men* as *CM*, and *Tripmaster Monkey* as *TM*.

8. See Lightfoot for an extensive exploration of dragon imagery and its implications for the narrative process in *The Woman Warrior*.

9. Kingston, in fact, notes its affinities to the American sitcom *I Love Lucy*: "The first half of the show is Lucy and Ethel. That's my mother and aunt, and they are stirring up everything. They are plotting to do something that will get their husbands into a lot of trouble" (Chin 58).

10. TuSmith notes that "the young protagonist's desire for easy answers when confronting her mother's 'talk-stories' is also the reader's need for firm ground on unfamiliar terrain" ("Literary Tricksterism" 253).

11. Kingston comments, "In a way, *The Woman Warrior* was a selfish book. I was always imposing my viewpoint on the stories. In *China Men* the person who 'talks story' is not so intrusive. . . . The more I was able to understand my characters, the more I was able to write from their point of view and the less interested I was in relating how I felt about them" (Pfaff 25).

12. Kingston's plea does in fact provoke a response: her father has answered by "writing poems and commentary in the margins of my books" ("Imagined" 565).

13. Kingston's representation of him here is significantly toned down; in *The Woman Warrior* her great uncle observes her and her sisters eating and shouts, "Maggot! Maggot! Maggot! Maggot! Maggot!" (191).

14. Li Ju-Chen, *Flowers in the Mirror*, trans. and ed. Lin Tai-Yi (London: Peter Owen, 1965).

15. See especially Goellnicht; and Cheung's discussion of *China Men* in *Articulate Silences.*

16. Charlotte Perkins Gilman uses a similar device in the opening of her feminist utopia, *Herland,* in which three male explorers who come upon a land of women are swiftly disabused of their preconceptions regarding women. Gilman, *Herland* (1915; reprint, New York: Pantheon, 1979).

17. I discuss Monkey, trickster protagonist of Wu Cheng-En's sixteenth-century novel *Journey to the West,* in greater detail later in this chapter.

18. Cheung comments that Ah Goong is "a ludic figure with a resilient and indomitable spirit, not unlike the famed title character in Lu Xun's *Ah Q* or the many tricksters in Native American writing" (*Articulate Silences* 105).

19. Linda Ching Sledge has noted his resemblance to "the wily Odysseus or the Nordic trickster Loki" (8).

20. This also curiously parallels an incident in *Tracks,* when Nanapush deliberately serves Pauline tea in order to force her to break her nun's vow of relieving herself only twice a day.

21. Typical of her cross-cultural interplay, Kingston presents this story of King Midas taken from Ovid's *Metamorphoses* as a traditional Chinese tale (Cheung, *Articulate Silences* 122).

22. Marilyn Yalom sees *The Woman Warrior* as postmodern, "*The Woman Warrior* as Postmodern Autobiography"; Patricia Lin and James Aubrey discuss *Tripmaster Monkey* as postmodern. In a review of *Tripmaster Monkey,* Gerald Vizenor calls Wittman a "postmodern monkey" ("Triumph" 1).

23. Hsia's introduction to *The Classic Chinese Novel* demonstrates the novel's origin both in an oral storytelling tradition and in written forms, especially historiography, which also tended to be rambling and episodic (Hsia 11). See also Feuerwerker, who corroborates the view of *Journey to the West* as repetitive and tedious, despite its "funny and irreverent" spirit and tone (174–178).

24. Amy Ling notes *Tripmaster Monkey*'s affinities to *Journey to the West* (147), Patricia Lin notes that Wittman's play is loosely based on *The Water Verge* (341), and James Aubrey remarks that Wittman stages *The Romance of the Three Kingdoms* (90).

25. Kingston's discovery of a pacifistic message in the war epic is a revisionist commentary on the growing trend in writing by Asian American men toward the glorification of the heroic martial tradition (see Cheung, "The Woman Warrior versus the Chinaman Pacific"). Wittman's conversion to pacifism through studying a war epic thus sends a message to proponents of that tradition to reevaluate the warlike values of the great heroic tradition.

26. See Aubrey for a more extensive treatment of this topic.

27. James Aubrey notes that "Wittman reworks violent materials for a peaceful end: the transformation of community" (95). The real solution, Kingston suggests, is not violence but a loving community.

28. Kingston mentions her narrator's resemblance to Kuan Yin in several interviews.

29. By calling the print medium gender- and color-blind, I do not refer to the human controllers of the publishing establishment, but to the paper and ink themselves.

30. Kenneth Price notes that Wittman himself is occasionally androgynous: PoPo repeatedly calls him "honey girl." Wittman's own revulsion against the stereotypic feminization of Chinese American men probably prevents Kingston from experimenting further with the androgyny of her trickster figure.

31. Kingston's emphasis on the healing powers of community—without idealizing the reality of that community—corresponds to the trend Bonnie TuSmith finds in ethnic works toward a literary expression of "the possibilities of communal healing" (*All My Relatives* 183).

32. "I do not propose to write an ode to dejection, but to brag as lustily as chanticleer in the morning, standing on his roost, if only to wake my neighbors up." Henry David Thoreau, epigraph to *Walden, or Life in the Woods*, ed. J. Lyndon Shanley (Princeton: Princeton UP, 1971).

33. Ellison argues that the trickster strategy of masking is inherently American (55).

34. She addressed this concern at an April 1989 conference at Tufts University.

CHAPTER THREE

1. The most extensive discussions of tricksters in Erdrich's work to date include those of James McKenzie, William Gleason, and Catherine Catt, especially Catt's "Ancient Myth in Modern America: The Trickster in the Works of Louise Erdrich." Though I agree with Catt's identification of tricksters as central to Erdrich's work, my reading of Erdrich's tricksters differs from hers. Catt stresses the trickster primarily as a mechanism for character development (76), whereas I see the trickster's influence as much more pervasive, particularly on the narrative level. In contrast to Catt's pan–Native American and even universalist analysis of the trickster, my reading draws mostly on Chippewa trickster traditions. As Erdrich's husband and collaborator, Michael Dorris, explains, "What Louise and I do is either within the context of a particular tribe or reservation or it is within the context of American literature" (H. Wong 198).

2. *Love Medicine* citations refer to the 1993 edition. In the text, *Love Medicine* will be cited as *LM*, *The Bingo Palace* as *BP*, *Tracks* as *T*, and *The Beet Queen* as *BQ*.

3. *Waynaboozhoo* is a less common variation of *Winabojo*, *Nanabooshoo*, or *Nanabozho*. Following Erdrich, who refers to the trickster once directly in *Love Medicine*, I use *Nanabozho* throughout.

4. Unlike the heaven of western thought, this afterlife is not exclusionary. Christopher Vecsey explains that "part of the happiness of the afterlife sprang from the fact that practically everyone went there" (64). The northern lights also figure prominently on the cover of *The Bingo Palace*, which shows them blazing over the lit-up bingo hall in a visual union of past and present, ancient myth and modern life.

5. Sarris specifically criticizes William Gleason's assertion that "Gerry IS Trickster, literally" (Sarris 61).

6. See Ruppert, "Mediation and Multiple Narrative" for a discussion of this tactic as a way of mediating between tribal, pan-tribal, and white audiences so that each audience learns something of the others' understanding of identity.

7. Gerald Vizenor recounts this and other adventures of Nanabozho in *The People Named the Chippewa*, 4–6.

8. Alan Velie notes that Vizenor also splits the trickster figure in *Darkness in St. Louis Bearheart* and that this practice is "not without precedent in myth and literature," citing for example Prometheus and Epimetheus in Greek mythology (131).

9. As James Flavin explains, *Tracks*'s oral context "heightens the tension within the text for it signals the potential for cultural survival or destruction. . . . When a child leaves [her] culture, when [she] dies or seeks other cultures within which to live, the entire community feels the loss" (3).

10. Nanapush's presence in the novel is so powerful that many critics seem to forget that half of the novel is narrated by Pauline Puyat; these critics call Nanapush the narrator or main character of *Tracks*. For readings of Nanapush as a trickster, see especially Flavin, Catt, and Bowers.

11. Debra Holt observes that "Nanapush outlives his blood relatives because he can read two sets of tracks—the ones left by animals in the woods and those left on paper" (160). Citing Nanapush's ability to read as a sign of his survival through adaptation, Catherine Catt pinpoints adaptability as the trickster's most valuable trait and explains that "Native American cultures, to survive in any form into the late twentieth century, have had to adapt to changing circumstances. . . . Trickster provides a model for establishing identity in the presence of change, for adapting, for surviving" (75).

12. Pauline Puyat, to whom I turn later, provides perhaps the most vivid example in Erdrich's fiction of the destruction this kind of identification can cause.

13. The Native American writer Greg Sarris identifies the combination of internalized racism and internalized oppression as the biggest problem of reservation life today and is troubled by its prevalence in Erdrich's books, wondering whether *Love Medicine* "treats the symptoms of a disease without getting at the cause" (142).

14. Erdrich's attitude toward Lyman is by no means wholly condemnatory. Her use of multiple perspectives allows comic cross-perspectives on all the characters. Here as elsewhere, Erdrich eschews judgment.

15. See Adamson-Clarke's discussion of Fleur as a "transformational" character.

16. Aside from Dot, who appears marginally in *Love Medicine* as Gerry's wife, Russell Kashpaw (*The Bingo Palace*), Dutch James (*Tracks*), and Fleur Pillager are the only connections between the novels, despite the fact that *The Beet Queen* and *Love Medicine* share roughly the same historical time frame.

17. This comic event also aligns her with Erdrich's other miracle worker, *Love Medicine*'s "Saint" Marie Kashpaw, whose hand wounds are revered as stigmata.

18. Karl's brother Jude experiences a similar collapse of identity years later at the Argus fair. Having arrived at the carnival to search for his family, the crowd's dispersion triggers his own breakdown: "All that held him together now was the crowd, and when the parade was finally over and they drew apart he would disperse too, in so many pieces that not even the work of his own clever hands could shape him back the way he was" (*BQ* 315).

19. Many of the chapters end on notes of dispersion, such as Celestine's conception of consciousness as "tiny bees, insects made of blue electricity, in a colony so fragile that it would scatter at the slightest touch" (*BQ* 204).

20. As I hope this study as a whole shows, this departure from other contemporary postmodern novels is something many women of color writers share. See Bonnie TuSmith's *All My Relatives* for a book-length study of the importance of community to ethnic writers.

21. This is, in fact, exactly the narrative situation in Nanapush's sections of *Tracks*, which are addressed specifically to Lulu with frequent reminders such as "This is where you come in, my girl, so listen" (*T* 57). Both Silberman and Kathleen Sands have noted that the orality of Erdrich's novels is innovative, deriving less from a sacred or ceremonial tradition than from the "secular anecdotal narrative process of community gossip" (Sands 12).

22. The extent to which an artistic orchestration of narrative voices can be genuinely healing has been the subject of debate in Erdrich criticism. Native American critics Gloria Bird and Greg Sarris both question the extent to which an artistic resolution is useful to those living on reservations. Sarris concedes, however, that "the fact that they are telling their stories, leading us through their pain to some resolution about it, means that . . . they do in fact have a way of talking about the pain" (133). Others, such as William Gleason and Sharon Manybeads Bowers, focus on the novels' humor as healing.

23. The 1993 *Love Medicine*, with its expanded sections on Lyman Lamartine and Gordie Kashpaw, greatly enhances the sense of conflict among contemporary community members.

24. See Peterson for an excellent discussion of *Tracks* as revisionist history.

25. Additions to the 1993 *Love Medicine* include one such important redefinition. After helping to deliver her daughter-in-law Marie's last child, Rushes Bear disowns her cheating, useless son Nector and names Marie her daughter (*LM* 104).

26. Erdrich even brings the myth into the revised version of *Love Medicine*. In joking reference to Nanabozho's gambling with the great gambler for his own spirit, Nanapush tells Lulu, "I lost my spirit to Father Damien six years ago, playing cards" (*LM* 71). Nanapush mentions this to Lulu while asking her to bury him in the traditional Chippewa manner, in a tree, which of course undercuts the idea that he has given up his Chippewa spirituality.

27. William Gleason explains that "laughter is not merely a by-product of survival, it is a critical force behind it. Faced with five

hundred years of physical, cultural, and spiritual genocide, Indians seek to steal power from their aggressors through inversion: by turning hatred into humor, the weakness of suffering is transformed into the strength of laughter" (66).

28. Bonnie TuSmith notes that Nanapush "doubles as a community historian/storyteller" in *Tracks*. In contrast, Pauline "speaks only for herself and speaks TO no one" (*All My Relatives* 130).

29. Michael, / The story comes up different / every time and has no ending / but always begins with you.

30. Erdrich and Dorris's collaboration process, as they have explained in numerous interviews, is essential to Erdrich's work and constitutes another tricksterlike aspect of her writing. Dorris comments in an interview that the collaboration process is like having an "opposite-gender version of yourself," perhaps the nearest human approach in storytelling to the trickster's androgyny (Bonetti 86).

31. Of course, as James Flavin observes, Nanapush's comment creates "an awkward moment in the text," in which "text threatens to subvert character. The name Nanapush, written upon the page, robs the character of power" (1).

32. Margaret (a.k.a. Rushes Bear) appears in the narratives of Lulu and Marie; Fleur, speaking in the old language, helps Marie through a dangerous childbirth; Moses figures prominently in Lulu's "The Island"; and Nanapush appears as vocally as ever in Lulu's remembrances.

33. My discussion invokes Gerald Vizenor's use of the phrase in *Narrative Chance: Postmodern Discourse on Native American Indian Literatures*. See especially his "Trickster Discourse" in *Narrative Chance*, discussed in chapter 1 of this volume.

34. Other third-person narrators include Albertine, Lyman, Shawnee, Redford, Gerry, Zelda, and—in a maneuver that momentarily takes us back to the early years of *Love Medicine*—the young June.

35. Erdrich commented in a radio interview that

We now have some of the biggest casinos in the Western hemisphere and there's a lot of controversy involved. A lot of good has come out of it; reservation roads, infrastructure, money for schools, jobs. . . . It used to be that people said "leave the reservation because you have to find opportunity," and now it's "come back because here is where you can get a job." My cousins are dealing blackjack. At the same time, . . . traditional values may erode; . . . an influx of people into the reservation may help further the loss of native languages and native culture. So it's a very shaky time for a lot of people. (Interview).

CHAPTER FOUR

1. Harris describes a "folk aura" that saturates Morrison's texts. In my view, the trickster's operation in language determines the narrative texture that Harris recognizes.

2. For recent historical analyses of the evolution of African American trickster tales, see Levine, Werner, Abrahams, and Roberts.

3. Although I mention Beloved here as part of this pattern, her complex relationship to African American history lies outside the scope of this chapter, which focuses on *Sula*, *Song of Solomon*, and *Tar Baby*.

4. Sula's identity challenges the possibility of her centrality as well: "she had no center, no speck around which to grow . . . no ego"(*TB* 119).

5. Although Shadrack as outsider does help shape community (his National Suicide Day becomes a part of local culture), unlike Sula "people understood the boundaries and nature of his madness" and "could fit him, so to speak, into the scheme of things" (*TB* 15). Shadrack's lunacy, because it is understood, represents less of a threat and therefore less of a community-shaping influence than does Sula's indefinable otherness.

6. In the text, *Sula* will be cited parenthetically as *S*, *Song of Solomon* as *SOS*, and *Tar Baby* as *TB*.

7. Thus, whereas Trudier Harris rightly remarks that Sula "carries no values that would sustain a society," her behavior does sustain the society, by challenging its values (*TB* 79).

8. For an alternative viewpoint on *Sula*'s relationship to the folk, see Harris, who suggests that the behavior of the Peace women in general reflects a folk world rather than a realistic one. (79)

9. Samuels and Hudson-Weems call her "trickster as hero" (77), and Gay Wilentz recognizes her as African trickster Legba (67).

10. The origin and associations of "tar women" will become clear in my subsequent discussion of *Tar Baby*, from which Denard draws this image.

11. Barbara Christian comments that Pilate "is so apart from the everyday world that her way cannot be the basis for transforming it. As heroic as she is, Pilate belongs to another time" ("Trajectories" 78).

12. Both Barbara Christian and Susan Blake call Pilate the spirit of her community (ibid.; Blake 78).

13. As Karen Carmean point out, the tree imagery often connected with Pilate also indicates her role as spiritual mediator: "in African mythology, trees often provide links between the living and spirit worlds, a role Pilate will fulfill" (21).

14. Milkman notes that in her late sixties Pilate has the "skin and agility of a teenaged girl," and Morrison comments that despite Pilate's death at the end of the novel, "Pilate is larger than life and never really dies. . . . She was not born, anyway—she gave birth to herself. So the question of her birth and death is irrelevant" (McKay, "Interview" 421).

15. *Tar Baby*, Morrison explains, "required whites because of the tar baby story. In the original story, the tar baby is made by a white man— that has to be the case with Jadine. . . . But the political statement [in *Tar Baby*] isn't as great to me as it is in *Song of Solomon*" (Wilson 128).

16. Sydney and Ondine's role in *Tar Baby*, as masking tricksters who compromise their pride and integrity in order to gain a measure of security, demonstrates the tensions inherent in this strategy. Mobley describes their masking strategies in Bakhtinian terms as "parodying themselves into carnivalesque figures" (*Folk Roots* 149).

17. See Skerrett for an extensive analysis of Pilate as griot.

18. This preface appeared in a special edition of *Tar Baby* (Franklin Center, Pa.: Franklin-Knopf, 1981).

19. For a fuller discussion of various versions of the "Tar Baby" story, see Harris's *Tar Baby* chapter in *Folklore and Fiction*.

20. Werner and Harris offer the most wide-ranging of such discussions.

21. Peter Erickson notes that "Jadine is an exception to the general rule of Morrison's infinite tolerance," noting that even child-abusers Margaret Street (*Tar Baby*) and Cholly Breedlove (*The Bluest Eye*) receive more sympathetic treatment than Jadine (301).

22. Her role as a Br'er Rabbit who has escaped a perilous, suffocating trap becomes clearer if we look at her story as an echo and revision of Nella Larsen's 1929 novel *Quicksand*. Like Jadine, Helga Crane is well educated, light-skinned, sought after by rich European men, and ambivalent about her own racial identity. Helga meets a black preacher, who like Son, is strongly rooted in African American folk culture. When Helga arrives in a southern rural community as the preacher's wife, she quickly becomes mired in the restrictive, smothering role, bearing baby after baby until childbirth kills her. Viewed in the light of Helga's story, Jadine has in some ways made a felicitous escape.

23. The limits of Therese's vision as storyteller also suggest why Morrison includes whites as psychologically realistic characters in her novel. Her own tricksterlike vision supersedes Therese's.

24. Although he distinguishes the appearance of tricksterlike figures (the rogue, clown, and fool) on the narrative and content levels of a novel, Bakhtin notes that (as in the case with Son) "quite often the two levels on which these images function come together into one" (163).

25. For a discussion of the dinner scene as a succession of mask removals, see Werner 160.

26. The importance of masks in African American literature and particularly in Tar Baby derives, according to Morrison, from the conviction of African Americans that "they are neither seen or listened to. They

also perceive themselves as morally superior people because they do SEE" (LeClair 376).

27. Morrison explains in an interview that in her view, the label "magical realism" implies a "diluted" realism and represents "a convenient way to skip . . . the truth in the art of certain writers." She explains, "My own use of enchantment simply comes because that's the way the world was for me and for the black people that I knew" (Christina Davis 414).

28. Elsewhere, she specifically defines the artist's role as communal: "a black artist for me, is not a solitary person who has no responsibility to the community. It's a total communal experience" (Christina Davis 419).

29. See Morrison, "Rootedness," for further discussion of her use of the chorus. There is an implied paradox in Morrison's linking of reader, community, and chorus; though the reader enters the book and community through its "holes and spaces," Morrison also writes the chorus, or communal reaction, into the book, thus guiding the form those "holes and spaces" should take.

30. For an excellent analysis of Morrison's use of African art forms, see Wilentz. Morrison herself repeatedly points out her work's affinity to other African American cultural forms, particularly the call-and-response, participatory features of African American spirituals and sermons and the improvisational nature of jazz (see McKay, "Interview" 426, 429).

31. What Susan Willis recognizes as "eruptions of funk" in Morrison's work signal the trickster's maneuvering behind the scenes to "shake up and disrupt" the reader's perceptions (Willis 323).

CHAPTER FIVE

1. In his new study, *Indi'n Humor*, Kenneth Lincoln asks the important question, "What about Coyote Old Woman? She has been slighted, if not slurred, in the myth-making of America, and now she snaps back

as a bushy-tailed, non-conformist, trickster Indian feminist" (174). Though his focus is specifically on Native American humor, Lincoln's work corresponds in many useful ways to my concept of a "trickster aesthetic." Drawing on Bakhtin, he suggests that the "polyphonic field of discourses, or 'voices,' from the subtexts . . . might better be seen as tricksterish 'inter-texts'—that is, tribal interplays of subject, object, audience, and time-space" (44).

2. Recent critics of African American folklore have been particularly vocal on this point, as the growing body of scholarship has focused on the continuity of African and African American traditions (see Roberts 6–14).

WORKS CITED

Abrahams, Roger D. *Afro-American Folk Tales*. New York: Pantheon, 1985.

Adamson-Clarke, Joni. "Transformation and Oral Tradition in Louise Erdrich's *Tracks*." *Studies in American Indian Literatures* 4.1 (1992): 28–48.

Allen, Paula Gunn. "'Border' Studies: The Intersection of Gender and Color." *Introduction to Scholarship in Modern Languages and Literatures*. Ed. Joseph Gibaldi. New York: MLA, 1992. 303–319.

———. "The Mythopoeic Vision in Native American Literature: The Problem of Myth." *American Indian Culture and Research Journal* 1 (1974): 1–13.

———. *The Sacred Hoop: Recovering the Feminine in American Indian Traditions*. Boston: Beacon Press, 1986.

Ammons, Elizabeth, and Annette White-Parks, eds. *Tricksterism in Turn-of-the-Century American Literature: A Multicultural Perspective*. Hanover: UP of New England, 1994.

Anzaldúa, Gloria. *Borderlands/La Frontera: The New Mestiza*. San Francisco: Aunt Lute Foundation, 1987.

Anzaldúa, Gloria, and Cherríe Moraga, eds. *This Bridge Called My Back: Radical Writings by Women of Color*. New York: Kitchen Table, Women of Color Press, 1983.

Aubrey, James R. "'Going toward War' in the Writings of Maxine Hong Kingston." *Vietnam Generation* 1.3–4 (1989): 90–101.

Baker, Houston A. "There Is No More Beautiful Way: Theory and the Poetics of Afro-American Women's Writing." *Afro-American Literary Study in the 1990s*. Ed. Houston A. Baker and Patricia Redmond. Chicago: U of Chicago P, 1989. 135–155.

Bakhtin, Mikhail. *The Dialogic Imagination: Four Essays by M. M. Bakhtin*. Ed. Michael Holquist. Austin: U of Texas P, 1981.

Ballinger, Franchot. "*Ambigere:* The Euro-American Picaro and the Native American Trickster." *MELUS* 17.1 (1992): 21–38.

Basso, Ellen. *In Favor of Deceit*. Tucson: U of Arizona P, 1987.

Bauer, Dale. *Feminist Dialogics: A Theory of Failed Community*. New York: SUNY Press, 1988.

Bauer, Dale, and S. Jaret Mckinstry, eds. *Feminism, Bakhtin, and the Dialogic*. New York: SUNY Press, 1991.

Beauvoir, Simone de. *The Second Sex*. 1952. Trans. and ed. H. M. Parshley. New York: Knopf, 1993.

Benton-Banai, Edward. *The Mishomis Book: The Voice of the Ojibway*. St. Paul, Minn.: Indiana Country Press, 1979.

Bevis, William. "Native American Novels: Homing In." *Recovering the Word: Essays on Native American Literature*. Ed. Brian Swann and Arnold Krupat. Berkeley: U of California P, 1987. 560–620.

Bird, Gloria. "Searching for Evidence of Colonialism at Work: A Reading of Louise Erdrich's *Tracks*." *Wicazo Sa Review* 8.2 (1992): 40–47.

Blake, Susan L. "Folklore and Community in *Song of Solomon*." *MELUS* 7.3 (1980): 77–82.

Bonetti, Kay. "Interview with Louise Erdrich and Michael Dorris." *Missouri Review* 11.2 (1988): 79–99.

Bowers, Sharon Manybeads. "Louise Erdrich as Nanapush." *New Perspectives on Women and Comedy*. Ed. Regina Barreca. Philadelphia: Gordon and Breach, 1992. 135–141.

Byerman, Keith E. "Beyond Realism." Gates and Appiah 100–125.

Carby, Hazel. *Reconstructing Womanhood*. New York: Oxford, 1987.

Carmean, Karen. *Toni Morrison's World of Fiction.* Troy, N.Y.: Whitston, 1993.

Catt, Catherine. "Ancient Myth in Modern America: The Trickster in the Works of Louise Erdrich." *Platte Valley Review* 19.1 (1991): 71–81.

Ch'eng-en, Wu. *Monkey.* Trans. Arthur Waley. London: Allen and Unwin, 1942.

Cheung, King-Kok. *Articulate Silences: Hisaye Yamamoto, Maxine Hong Kingston, Joy Kogawa.* Ithaca: Cornell UP, 1993.

———. "Don't Tell: Imposed Silences in *The Color Purple* and *The Woman Warrior.*" *PMLA* 103.2 (1988): 162–174.

———. "The Woman Warrior versus the Chinaman Pacific: Must a Chinese American Critic Choose between Feminism and Heroism?" *Conflicts in Feminism.* Ed. Marianne Hirsch and Evelyn Fox Keller. New York: Routledge, 1990. 234–251.

Chin, Frank. *The Chinaman Pacific & Frisco R.R. Co.* Minneapolis: Coffee House Press, 1988.

———. "Come All Ye Asian American Writers of the Real and the Fake." *The Big Aiiieeeee!: An Anthology of Chinese American and Japanese American Literature.* Ed. Jeffery Paul Chan et al. New York: Meridian, 1974. 1–92.

Chin, Marilyn. "A *MELUS* Interview: Maxine Hong Kingston." *MELUS* 16.4 (1989–1990): 57–74.

Christian, Barbara. *Black Feminist Criticism.* New York: Pergamon, 1985.

———. "Trajectories of Self-Definition: Placing Contemporary Afro-American Women's Fiction." Pryse and Spillers 233–248.

Chua, Cheng Lok. "Mythopoesis East and West in *The Woman Warrior.*" Lim 146–150.

Coleman, James. "The Quest for Wholeness in Toni Morrison's *Tar Baby.*" *Black American Literature Forum* 20.1–2 (1986): 63–74.

Darling, Marsha. "In the Realm of Responsibility: A Conversation with Toni Morrison." *Women's Review of Books* 5 (March 1988): 5–6.

Dasenbrock, Reed Way. "Intelligibility and Meaningfulness in Multicultural Literature in English." *PMLA.* 102.1 (1987): 10–19.

Davis, Christina. "Interview with Toni Morrison." Gates and Appiah 412–420.

Davis, Cynthia A. "Self, Society, and Myth in Toni Morrison's Fiction." *Modern Critical Views: Toni Morrison.* Ed. Harold Bloom. New York: Chelsea House, 1990. 7–26.

Denard, Carolyn. "The Convergence of Feminism and Ethnicity in the Fiction of Toni Morrison." McKay 171–179.

Densmore, Frances. *Chippewa Customs.* St. Paul: Minnesota Historical Society Press, 1979.

Doty, William, and William Hynes, eds. *Mythical Trickster Figures.* Tuscaloosa: U of Alabama P, 1993.

Doueihi, Anne. "Inhabiting the Space between Discourse and Story in Trickster Narratives." Doty and Hynes 193–201.

Ellison, Ralph. *Shadow and Act.* New York: Random House, 1964.

Erdrich, Louise. *The Beet Queen.* New York: Bantam, 1986.

———. *The Bingo Palace.* New York: HarperPerennial, 1994.

———. Interview. *Morning Edition.* National Public Radio. KERA, Dallas. 11 Jan. 1994.

———. *Love Medicine.* Expanded ed. New York: HarperPerennial, 1993.

———. *Tracks.* New York: Harper and Row, 1989.

———. "Where I Ought to Be: A Writer's Sense of Place." *New York Times* 28 July 1985, sec. 7: 1+.

Erickson, Peter B. "Images of Nurturance in *Tar Baby*." Gates and Appiah 293–307.

Felski, Rita. *Beyond Feminist Aesthetics.* Cambridge: Harvard UP, 1989.

Feuerwerker, Yi-Tse Mei. "The Chinese Novel." *Approaches to the Oriental Classics.* Ed. Wm. Theodore de Bary. Morningside Heights, N.Y.: Columbia UP, 1958.

Fischer, Michael M. J. "Ethnicity and the Post-Modern Arts of Memory." *Writing Culture: The Poetics and Politics of Ethnography.* Ed. James Clifford and George E. Marcus. Berkeley: U of California P, 1986. 194–233.

Fishkin, Shelley Fisher. "Interview with Maxine Hong Kingston." *American Literary History* 3.4 (1991): 782–791.

Flavin, James. "The Novel as Performance: Communication in Louise Erdrich's *Tracks.*" *Studies in American Indian Literature* 3.2 (1991): 1–12.

Frye, Northrop. *Anatomy of Criticism.* Princeton: Princeton UP, 1957.

———. "The Archetypes of Literature." *Myth and Literature: Contemporary Theory and Practice.* Ed. John B. Vickery. Lincoln: U of Nebraska P, 1986.

Gates, Henry Louis, Jr. *Figures in Black: Words, Signs, and the "Racial" Self.* New York: Oxford UP, 1987.

———. *The Signifying Monkey.* New York: Oxford UP, 1988.

Gates, Henry Louis, Jr., and K. A. Appiah, eds. *Toni Morrison: Critical Perspectives Past and Present.* New York: Amistad, 1993.

Gilligan, Carol. *In a Different Voice: Psychological Theory and Women's Development.* Cambridge: Harvard UP, 1982.

Gleason, William. "'Her Laugh an Ace': The Function of Humor in Louise Erdrich's *Love Medicine.*" *American Indian Culture and Research Journal* 11.3 (1987): 51–73.

Goellnicht, Donald C. "Tang Ao in America: Male Subject Positions in *China Men.*" Lim and Ling 191–212.

Gotera, Vicente F. "'I've Never Read Anything Like It': Student Responses to *The Woman Warrior.*" Lim 64–73.

Harris, Trudier. *Fiction and Folklore in the Novels of Toni Morrison.* Knoxville: U of Tennessee P, 1991.

Henderson, Mae Gwendolyn. "Speaking in Tongues: Dialogics, Dialectics, and the Black Woman Writer's Literary Tradition." *Changing Our Own Words: Essays on Criticism, Theory, and Writing by Black Women.* Ed. Cheryl A. Wall. New Brunswick: Rutgers UP, 1989.

Holt, Debra. "Transformation and Continuance: Native American Tradition in the Novels of Louise Erdrich." *Entering the 90s: The North American Experience.* Sault Sainte Marie, Mich.: Lake Superior State UP, 1991.

hooks, bell. *Feminist Theory from Margin to Center.* Boston: South End Press, 1984.

———. *Yearning: Race, Gender, and Cultural Politics.* Boston: South End Press, 1990.

Hower, Edward. "Magic Recaptured: Review of Erdrich's *The Bingo Palace.*" *Wall Street Journal* 4 Jan. 1994, Leisure and Arts.

Hsia, C. T. *The Classic Chinese Novel.* New York: Columbia UP, 1968.

Hunt, Linda. "I Could Not Figure Out What Was My Village": Gender versus Ethnicity in Maxine Hong Kingston's *The Woman Warrior.*" *MELUS* 12.3 (1985): 5–12.

Hynes, William. "Inconclusive Conclusions: Tricksters—Metaplayers and Revealers." Doty and Hynes 202–217.

———. "Mapping the Characteristics of Mythic Tricksters: A Heuristic Guide." Doty and Hynes 33–45.

Iser, Wolfgang. "Interaction between Text and Reader." Suleiman and Crosman 105–114.

———. *The Implied Reader.* Baltimore: Johns Hopkins UP, 1974.

Islas, Arturo. "Maxine Hong Kingston: Interview with Arturo Islas." *Women Writers of the West Coast: Speaking Their Lives and Careers.* Ed. Marilyn Yalom. Santa Barbara: Capra Press, 1983.

Johansen, Ruthann Knechel. *The Narrative Secret of Flannery O'Connor: The Trickster as Interpreter.* Tuscaloosa: U of Alabama P, 1994.

Johnston, Basil. *Ojibway Heritage.* New York: Columbia UP, 1976.

Jones, Ann Rosalind. "Inscribing Femininity: French Theories of the Feminine." *Making a Difference: Feminist Literary Criticism.* Ed. Gayle Greene and Coppelia Kahn. New York: Methuen, 1985.

Jones, Gayl. *Liberating Voices: Oral Tradition in African American Literature.* Cambridge: Harvard UP, 1991.

Jung, Carl J. "On the Psychology of the Trickster Figure." *The Trickster: A Study of American Indian Mythology.* By Paul Radin. New York: Philosophical Library, 1956.

Kehde, Suzanne. "Voices from the Margin: Bag Ladies and Others." Bauer and Mckinstry 25–38.

Kim, Elaine. Foreword. Lim and Ling xi–xvii.

———. "'Such Opposite Creatures': Men and Women in Asian American Literature." *Michigan Quarterly Review* 24.1 (1990): 68–93.

Kingston, Maxine Hong. "Cultural Mis-Readings by American Reviewers." *Asian and Western Writers in Dialogue: New Cultural Identities.* Ed. Guy Amirthanayagam. London: Macmillan, 1982. 55–65.

———. "Imagined Life." *Michigan Quarterly Review* 22 (1983): 561–570.

———. "Personal Statement." Lim 23–25.

———. *Tripmaster Monkey.* New York: Vintage, 1989.

———. *The Woman Warrior.* New York: Vintage, 1989.

Knapp, Bettina L. *A Jungian Approach to Literature. Carbondale:* Southern Illinois UP, 1984

Larsen, Nella. *Quicksand* and *Passing.* New Brunswick: Rutgers UP, 1986.

Lauter, Estella. *Women as Mythmakers.* Bloomington: Indiana UP, 1984.

LeClair, Thomas. "The Language Must Not Sweat: A Conversation with Toni Morrison." Gates and Appiah 369–377.

Lee, Robert G. "*The Woman Warrior* as Intervention in Asian American Historiography." Lim 52–63.

Lenz, William E. *Fast Talk and Flush Times.* Columbia: U of Missouri P, 1985.

Levine, Lawrence W. "'Some Go Up and Some Go Down': The Meaning of the Slave Trickster." *The Hofstadter Aegis, A Memorial.* Ed. Stanley Elkins. New York: Knopf, 1974. 94–124.

Li, David Leiwei. "*China Men:* Maxine Hong Kingston and the American Canon." *American Literary History* 3.2 (1990): 482–502.

———. "The Naming of a Chinese American 'I': Cross-Cultural Sign/ifications in *The Woman Warrior.*" *Criticism* 30.4 (1988): 497–515.

Lightfoot, Marjorie J. "Hunting the Dragon in Kingston's *The Woman Warrior.*" *MELUS* 13.3–4: 55–66.

Lim, Shirley Geok-Lin. "The Ambivalent American: Asian American Literature on the Cusp." Lim and Ling 13–32.

Lim, Shirley Geok-Lin, ed. *Approaches to Teaching "The Woman Warrior."* New York: MLA, 1991.

Lim, Shirley Geok-Lin, and Amy Ling, eds. *Reading the Literatures of Asian America*. Philadelphia: Temple UP, 1992.

Lin, Patricia. "Clashing Constructs of Reality: Reading Maxine Hong Kingston's *Tripmaster Monkey: His Fake Book* as Indigenous Ethnography." Lim and Ling 333–346.

Lincoln, Kenneth. *Indi'n Humor: Bicultural Play in Native America*. New York: Oxford UP, 1993.

Lindberg, Gary. *The Confidence Man in American Literature*. New York: Oxford UP, 1982.

Ling, Amy. *Between Worlds: Women Writers of Chinese Ancestry*. New York: Pergamon Press, 1990.

McKay, Nellie. "An Interview with Toni Morrison." Gates and Appiah 413–429.

McKay, Nellie, ed. *Critical Essays on Toni Morrison*. Boston: G. K. Hall, 1988.

McKenzie, James. "Lipsha's Good Road Home: The Revival of Chippewa Culture in *Love Medicine*." *American Indian Culture and Research Journal* 10.3 (1986): 53–63.

Minh-ha, Trinh T. *Woman, Native, Other: Writing Postcoloniality and Feminism*. Indianapolis: Indiana UP, 1989.

Mobley, Marilyn Sanders. *Folk Roots and Mythic Wings in Sara Orne Jewett and Toni Morrison*. Baton Rouge: Louisiana State UP, 1991.

———. "Narrative Dilemma: Jadine as Cultural Orphan in *Tar Baby*." Gates and Appiah 284–292.

Morrison, Toni. "Memory, Creation, and Writing." *Thought* 59.235 (1984): 385–390.

———. Preface. *Tar Baby*. By Morrison. Franklin, Pa.: Franklin-Knopf, 1981.

———. "Rootedness: The Ancestor as Foundation." *Black Women Writers (1950–1980): A Critical Evaluation*. Ed. Mari Evans. Garden City, N.Y.: Anchor Press, 1984. 339–345.

———. *Song of Solomon*. New York: Signet, 1978.

———. *Tar Baby*. 1981. New York: Signet, 1983.

———. "Unspeakable Things Unspoken: The Afro-American Presence in American Literature." *Michigan Quarterly Review* 28 (1989): 1–34.

Newton, Judith, and Deborah Rosenfelt, eds. *Feminist Criticism and Social Change.* New York: Methuen, 1985.

Nishime, LeiLani. "Engendering Genre: Gender and Nationalism in *China Men* and *The Woman Warrior.*" *MELUS* 20.1 (1995): 67–82.

Oakes, Karen. "Reading Trickster; or, Theoretical Reservations and a Seneca Tale." Ammons and White-Parks 137–157.

O'Connor, Mary. "Subject, Voice, and Women in Some Contemporary Black American Women's Writing." Bauer and Mckinstry 199–217.

Ostriker, Alicia. "Thieves of Language: Women Poets and Revisionist Mythmaking." *The New Feminist Criticism.* Ed. Elaine Showalter. New York: Pantheon, 1985. 314–338.

Pelton, Robert D. *The Trickster in West Africa: A Study of Mythic Irony and Sacred Delight.* Berkeley: U of California P, 1980.

Perez-Castillo, Susan. "Postmodernism, Native American Literature, and the Real: The Silko-Erdrich Controversy." *Massachusetts Review* 32.2 (1991): 285–294.

Peterson, Nancy J. "History, Postmodernism, and Louise Erdrich's *Tracks.*" *PMLA* 109.5 (1994): 982–994.

Pfaff, Timothy. "Talk with Mrs. Kingston." *New York Times Book Review* 15 June 1980: 25+.

Pratt, Annis. *Archetypal Patterns in Women's Fiction.* Bloomington: Indiana UP, 1981.

Price, Kenneth. "Rethinking Whitman in Kingston's *Tripmaster Monkey.*" Paper presented at MELUS Conference, U of California. Berkeley, 30 April 1993.

Price Herndl, Diane. "The Dilemmas of a Feminine Dialogic." Bauer and Mckinstry 7–24.

Pryse, Marjorie, and Hortense J. Spillers, eds. *Conjuring: Black Women, Fiction, and Literary Tradition.* Bloomington: Indiana UP, 1985.

Rabinowitz, Paula. "Naming, Magic, and Documentary: The Subversion of the Narrative in *Song of Solomon, Ceremony,* and *China Men.*"

Feminist Re-Visions. Ed. Vivian Patraka and Louise Tilly. Ann Arbor: U of Michigan P, 1983. 26–42.

Radin, Paul. *The Trickster: A Study in American Indian Mythology.* New York: Schocken, 1956.

Rainwater, Catherine. "Reading between Worlds: Narrativity in the Fiction of Louise Erdrich." *American Literature* 62.3 (1990): 405–422.

Roberts, John W. *From Trickster to Badman: The Black Folk Hero in Slavery and Freedom.* Philadelphia: U of Pennsylvania P, 1989.

Ruppert, James. "Mediation and Multiple Narrative in Contemporary Native American Fiction." *Texas Studies in Literature and Language* 28.2 (1986): 209–225.

Rushkin, Donna Kate. "The Bridge Poem." Anzaldúa and Moraga xxi–xxii.

Sale, Maggie. "Call and Response as Critical Method: African American Oral Traditions in Beloved." *African American Review* 26.1 (1992): 41–50.

Samuels, Wilfred, and Clenora Hudson-Weems. *Toni Morrison.* Boston: Twayne, 1990.

Sands, Kathleen. Review of *Love Medicine. Studies in American Indian Literatures* 9.1 (1985): 12–24.

Sarris, Greg. *Keeping Slug Woman Alive: A Holistic Approach to American Indian Texts.* Berkeley: U of California P, 1993.

Schueller, Malini. "Questioning Race and Gender Definitions: Dialogic Subversions in *The Woman Warrior.*" *Criticism* 31.4 (1989): 421–437.

Silberman, Robert. "Opening the Text: *Love Medicine* and the Return of the Native American Woman." Vizenor 101–121.

Skerrett, Joseph T., Jr. "Recitation to the *Griot:* Storytelling and Learning in Toni Morrison's *Song of Solomon.* Pryse and Spillers 192–202.

Sledge, Linda Ching. "Maxine Kingston's *China Men:* The Family Historian as Epic Poet." *MELUS* 7.4 (1980): 3–29.

Slotkin, Richard. "Myth and the Production of History." *Ideology and Classic American Literature.* Ed. Sacvan Bercovitch and Myra Jehlen. Cambridge: Cambridge UP, 1986. 70–90.

Smith, Jeanne R. "Transpersonal Selfhood: The Boundaries of Identity in Louise Erdrich's *Love Medicine*." *Studies in American Indian Literatures* 3.4 (1991): 13–26.

St. Hilaire, Joanne. "*Tracks*, a Trickster Novel." Paper presented at American Women Writers of Color Conference. Salisbury State, Maryland, June 1993.

Stepto, Robert B. "'Intimate Things in Place': A Conversation with Toni Morrison." Gates and Appiah 378–395.

Stripes, James D. "The Problem(s) of (Anishinaabe) History in the Fiction of Louise Erdrich: Voices and Contexts." *Wicazo-Sa Review* 7.2 (1991): 26–33.

Suleiman, Susan, and Inge Crosman, eds. "Interaction between Text and Reader." *The Implied Reader*. Princeton: Princeton UP, 1980. 105–114.

Tate, Claudia. "A Conversation with Toni Morrison." *Black Women Writers at Work*. New York: Continuum, 1983. 117–131.

Thompson, Phyllis Hoge. "This Is the Story I Heard: A Conversation with Maxine Hong Kingston and Earll Kingston." *Biography* 6.1 (1983): 1–12.

Traylor, Eleanor. "The Fabulous World of Toni Morrison: *Tar Baby*." McKay 135–149.

Turner, Victor. "Myth and Symbol." *The International Encyclopedia of Social Sciences*. New York: Macmillan, 1968. 576–582.

———. *The Ritual Process*. Ithaca: Cornell UP, 1977.

TuSmith, Bonnie. *All My Relatives: Community in Contemporary Ethnic American Literatures*. Ann Arbor: U of Michigan P, 1993.

———. "Literary Tricksterism: Maxine Hong Kingston's *The Woman Warrior*." *Literature, Interpretation, Theory: LIT* 2 (1991): 249–259.

Van Dyke, Annette. "Questions of the Spirit: Bloodlines in Louise Erdrich's Chippewa Landscape." *Studies in American Indian Literatures* 4.1 (1992): 15–27.

Vecsey, Christopher. *Traditional Ojibwa Religion and Its Historical Changes*. Philadelphia: American Philosophical Society, 1983.

Velie, Alan. "The Trickster Novel." Vizenor 121–139.

Vizenor, Gerald. *The People Named the Chippewa*. Minneapolis: U of Minnesota P, 1984.

———. "Trickster Discourse." Vizenor 187–211.

———. *The Trickster of Liberty: Tribal Heirs to a Wild Baronage*. Minneapolis: U of Minnesota P, 1988.

———. "The Triumph of Monkey Business." *Los Angeles Times Book Review* 23 April 1989: 1, 13.

Vizenor, Gerald, ed. *Narrative Chance: Postmodern Discourse on Native American Indian Literatures*. Albuquerque: U of New Mexico P, 1989.

Wadlington, Warwick. *The Confidence Game in American Literature*. Princeton: Princeton UP, 1975.

Watkins, Mel. "Talk with Toni Morrison." *New York Times Magazine* 11 Sept. 1977: 48, 50.

Werner, Craig H. "The Briar Patch as Modernist Myth: Morrison, Barthes, and Tar Baby As-Is." McKay 150–167.

Wiget, Andrew. "His Life in His Tail: The Native American Trickster and the Literature of Possibility." *Redefining American Literary History*. Ed. A. LaVonne Brown Ruoff and Jerry W. Ward Jr. New York: MLA, 1990. 83–96.

Wilentz, Gay. "Civilizations Underneath: African Heritage as Cultural Discourse in Toni Morrison's *Song of Solomon*." *African American Review* 26.1 (1992): 61–76.

Willis, Susan. "Eruptions of Funk: Historicizing Toni Morrison." Gates and Appiah 308–329.

Wilson, Judith. "A Conversation with Toni Morrison." *Essence* July 1981: 84+.

Wolfe, Bernard. "Uncle Remus and the Malevolent Rabbit: 'Takes a Limber-Toe Gemmun fer ter Jump Jim Crow.'" 1949. *Critical Essays on Joel Chandler Harris*. Ed. R. Bruce Bickley Jr. Boston: G. K. Hall, 1981. 70–84.

Wong, Hertha D. "Interview with Louise Erdrich and Michael Dorris." *North Dakota Quarterly* 55.1 (1987): 196–218.

Wong, Sau-ling Cynthia. "Necessity and Extravagance in Maxine Hong Kingston's *Woman Warrior:* An Inquiry into the Nature of Art and Its Relevance to the Ethnic Experience." *MELUS* 15.1 (1988): 44–66.

Woo, Deborah. "Maxine Hong Kingston: The Ethnic Writer and the Burden of Dual Authenticity." *Amerasia* 16.1 (1990): 173–200.

Yalom, Marilyn. "*The Woman Warrior* as Postmodern Autobiography." Lim 108–115.

Yu, Anthony C., trans. and ed. *The Journey to the West.* 3 vols. Chicago: U of Chicago P, 1977.

Zagarell, Sandra. "Narrative of Community: The Identification of a Genre." *Signs* 13.3 (1988): 498–527.

INDEX

Compositor:	BookMasters, Inc.
Text:	10/15 Janson
Display:	Janson
Printer and binder:	Haddon Craftsmen, Inc.